SUPERPOWERS

Mark A. Radcliffe is the author of two novels, *Gabriel's Angel* (2010) and *Stranger Than Kindness* (2013), both published by Bluemoose Books. He has worked as a singer, mental health nurse, journalist and Senior Lecturer in Health Care. He is currently the Subject Lead for Creative Writing at West Dean College of Art and Conservation, Chichester.

Beyond all that he likes to swim in very cold water, has written a column for *The Nursing Times* for twenty-five years and grows vegetables to give to strangers – because you can tell a lot about a society by how it responds to free home-grown veg. He lives in Hove, East Sussex with his wife Kate, and daughter, Maia.

Superpowers

MARK A. RADCLIFFE

VP

Valley Press

First published in 2020 by Valley Press
Woodend, The Crescent, Scarborough, YO11 2PW
www.valleypressuk.com

ISBN 978-1-912436-45-3
Cat. no. VP0165

Cover illustration by Ben Hardaker.
Cover design by Jamie McGarry.
Text design by Steve Foot.

Printed and bound in the EU by Pulsio, Paris.

Contents

Dedicated to Cecilia Radcliffe, 1924-2015

"The truth is the thing I invented so I could live."
— Nicole Krauss, *The History of Love*

ACKNOWLEDGEMENTS

With thanks to Kim Goddard, Kate and
Maia Radcliffe, Bonnie Azab Powell, Tilly Bones, George
the cat (RIP), and Jamie, Tess and Sam at Valley Press.

The Woman Who Could Talk with Cats or, if you prefer, Catwoman

T HIS IS A story about wanting – actually, trying – to share a secret. I thought it was going to be a story about a remarkable gift, but it turns out it isn't. I can talk with cats. The important word here is 'with'. Obviously I can talk to cats. Everyone can talk to cats in the same way that they talk to babies, vegetables, and to their God. But when I talk to cats they invariably talk back. Unless they are sulking. Or busy. Or eating.

I am not mad. I work as a psychiatrist and, to put it bluntly, I have done all the tests. Apart from the cat conversations and a brief self-punishing and rageful relationship with food when I was fourteen, I am quite normal – whatever normal is. I don't have a very active social life, in part because being able to talk with cats is not something one shares comfortably with other people, and so I always feel as though I am withholding in my relationships. That was harder when I was young, particularly in that thrill of a new friendship where you want to share secrets. There could be a lull and I would want to say, 'I can talk with cats…' but I never did. I never told a soul. Although, having said that, cats know and I have no idea who else they may have told. I certainly believe they tell other cats.

My parents died when I was very young. My father was run over by a drunk driver when I was five, my mother drowned when I was nine. It may have been on purpose. I suspect it was. When I think of her all I can remember is the darkness that accompanied her all of the time, and so I don't think about my mother very much at all.

I spent time in a care home, which can be isolating, particularly if you are, as I was, a quiet and bookish child. That's where I first made friends with a cat. His name was Herbie. He was ginger. He spoke to me for the first time on my eleventh birthday. He said I would be fostered before I turned twelve. He was a clever cat – he could talk – but he was no clairvoyant. I wasn't fostered until I was nearly thirteen. It didn't last.

I survived. Mostly one does. Schoolwork was my sanctuary. I would have loved to have been a musician but there is a limit to what you can do without lessons. I play piano, guitar and a little clarinet. I always wanted to learn the harp. I taught myself, quietly. I was never encouraged to play. Cats don't like music.

After A-levels I won a scholarship. I was on the local news for nearly fifteen seconds – a symbol of social mobility. I was not unfamiliar with the glare of the media. I had my photograph taken with the local MP after my GCSEs. He put his arm around me, and when he took it away he quite slowly and methodically brushed his hand across my bottom. He smelt of mint and bitter aftershave. There was a cat who belonged – in so far as a cat ever belongs – to the school caretaker, who I spoke with occasionally. I told him I was embarrassed. He asked why. I said it was because I knew that the man was sordid and inappropriate and that he was probably capable, in circumstances that enabled him, of assault. 'And?' the cat asked.

'I am embarrassed,' I whispered, 'because if his hand had lingered, I would not have pushed it away. Not out of desire or fear but because I was curious.'

It was a curiosity I chose not to attend to for the next fifteen years.

I was, throughout my Cambridge years, appropriately demure. I was friendly but reserved and quiet. I had friends but nobody very close. Nobody I shared secrets with. Well, there were a couple of cats I got on well with. One of them wrote poetry. When I say write I mean made up and recited. Cats don't write, although he did like to dictate.

I graduated. I specialised in psychiatry. I worked. I attended ward nights out, but being present and peripheral is not a difficult skill to master. Dress as though you are ten years older than you are and wear dull shoes; that is the way to stay separate. I built my isolation from the feet upwards.

However, there came a point, or a man, when finally I had to take a chance. I knew that in order to share my secret I was going to need the cats' help. On the face of it, one might think that would be quite straight forward. Cats and I talk, why wouldn't they help? But that presumes that cats care about my ability to understand them. And it assumes they have a capacity or even a desire to do favours. Animals do not casually exchange good deeds. They do not have complex or morally-constructed relations. Indeed, cats – unlike dogs – do not even do tricks for treats; they can't be easily bribed. We ascribe them a dignity or aloofness because of this but in truth they are cats. Negotiation is no more available to them than licking the backs of our legs is to us.

A couple of years ago I met Daniel. He was a nurse who came to work on one of my wards. I liked him immediately. He was good-looking and quietly confident, and he smiled when he spoke without looking sarcastic. I am not a naturally confident woman but I got the sense he quite liked me. Even so, it took what seemed like ages for him to ask me out.

I know what you are thinking: why didn't I ask him out? That's what the cats said. But it's difficult. I am a doctor and he is a nurse. That makes things complicated. And anyway, I am naturally shy. I am friendly with cats. Think about it.

There is a cat who lives three doors down. I should say at this point that I don't own a cat. It would feel oppressive. Anyway, this cat, who called himself Bob, even though his keepers referred to him as Freckle, became my confidant around this time. I remember telling him about Daniel, saying I was preoccupied with him and had started listening to late-night jazz music. I didn't think I liked jazz music.

'It does tend to meander,' said Bob.

'I'm twenty-nine,' I would say.

'What is that in cat years?' asked Bob.

'Nearly five.'

'Prime of life,' said Bob.

'Exactly,' I said. 'But I feel about fourteen – or about two in cat years.'

'Two? You are very distractible at two. Still sometimes taken in by big wool,' said Bob.

'It feels like when you have a crush…'

'Have you considered rolling onto your back and spreading your paws?'

'I'm not a cat.'

'I'm sorry,' said Bob. 'It's just that you speak such good cat.'

Finally Daniel asked me out. We went for a drink and a pizza. I didn't want him to think I ate too much so I made myself a tuna sandwich before I went out. But then he seemed worried that I didn't like pizza, so I ate more than I needed and felt a bit bloated. Again, it was just like when I was fourteen.

He blushed when he said he had liked me for some time, but that he was sensitive to the fact that he was a nurse and I was a doctor. That made him seem charming, human even.

We went back to his place, a one-bedroom housing association flat in Portslade. It was full of books and records and a surprising number of shoes. It could have turned out badly but it didn't. He smelt of sandalwood and cheese. He laughed at my jokes in the right places. He fell asleep holding my elbow in the palm of his hand. And he didn't own a cat.

So Daniel became the first person I wanted to tell about the cats.

I told Bob.

Bob said, 'I know a cat who can help.' That's how I met George. In the world of cats I think he was something of a fixer.

A few days later Daniel came around to my house. He brought wine and flowers. You know you are in trouble when you catch your breath in the face of a cliché. I have been buying myself flowers every Friday evening for eight years. I only have one vase. I put his flowers in a milk jug some friends had bought me for my 21st birthday. I pretended that was what I used it for.

I was nervous and it showed. He probably thought my anxiety was born of it being a date, or my having to cook, or the fact that I embodied awkwardness whenever I was not being a psychiatrist. In truth it was because I felt I was about to spill my secret into the world for the first time and that would make me more vulnerable than I had ever been. Or worse, I was going to demonstrate to myself that I was unlovable. Because of the cats.

We drank a bottle of wine before we ate, and we drank a second during dinner. I was drunk and emotional. He was funny and kissable.

'I didn't know you had a cat,' he said.

'I don't.' I turned around and there was George.

'George,' I said.

'Evening,' he said. 'Have you told him?'

I shook my head.

When I see a cat sitting upright, I am always struck by how aligned their front paws are. I wondered if they do that on purpose or if it just happens. I may have been looking for a distraction.

'How do you do that with your paws, George?' I asked.

'Do what?' said George.

'Make them so perfectly aligned.'

George looked down and padded the carpet.

'It just happens.'

'Blimey,' said Daniel. 'It's like he knew what you were talking about then.'

I smiled. 'I think you are using my paws to distract you from the issue at hand. You people do that sort of thing quite a lot,' said George.

I nodded. 'You are right, of course.'

'Now might be a good time,' said George.

I took a deep breath and turned to Daniel. 'Do you believe in superpowers?'

'What, like Spiderman?'

I shrugged.

'Not really my thing. Why do you ask?'

'Well, because I have a ... quirk.' The word 'quirk' came out wrong, louder at the end. It emphasised the fact that I was quite full of wine.

He raised his eyebrows. I couldn't tell if it was flirtatious and he imagined I was about to reveal sexual preferences before pudding, or he was letting me know I was drunk.

'I'm not being sexual,' I said clumsily.

He smiled and nodded.

'Daniel, I can talk with cats and the cats talk back. I know, absolutely insane. Get your coat, hit the road, Nina

14

is la-la. You know psychotic when you sleep with it, blah blah blah.'

'You people are weird,' said George.

'Not now, George,' I said.

Daniel was looking at me half smiling, waiting for the punch line.

I took a deep breath. 'Look, can I show you something, please?'

Daniel nodded and I turned to George.

'I'm not doing any tricks,' George said. And then he sighed and added, 'Ask him to say a number between five and seventy-five.'

'Say a number between five and seventy-five,' I said to Daniel. 'Please.'

'Sixty-two,' he said.

'Sixty-two,' I said.

'Sixty-two,' nodded George. 'I'll be back as soon as I can. Give me fifteen minutes and then take him upstairs and look out of the back window.'

'You are not going to find sixty-two cats in fifteen minutes,' I said, but George was gone. Cats are quick when they want to be.

Daniel, quite understandably, had the look of a man whose evening had taken an unexpected turn.

'I need you to come upstairs,' I said to Daniel.

He raised his eyebrows but it was half-hearted. I smiled. 'I know,' I said. 'Humour me.'

We went upstairs. Not in the manner I had anticipated earlier in the evening. It was more of a trudge. 'Are we going to see sixty-two cats in the garden?' asked Daniel.

I shrugged as we entered the back bedroom. The back bedroom exists for guests. It has never been used. It is sparse and is the only room in the house with curtains instead of blinds. It smelled a bit like damp, although I suspect it was more the musty smell you get when rooms have been empty for a long time. To his credit, as we stood in the darkened room looking out of the window into the moonlit garden, Daniel gently stroked the inside of my arm. It was tender and it made me want to cry.

Then George appeared. At first he sat in the garden on his own, but soon he was joined by Bob, then two other cats I didn't know. Then more cats came, in twos and threes from different directions. I had never seen so many cats gather in one place so quickly. Daniel said 'wow' and he held my arm. There were a lot of cats but not sixty-two. Nowhere near.

I looked at Daniel. He had the softest eyes I had ever seen on a man. Brown, unclouded and so beautifully open. 'I make it about twenty-three cats,' I said.

'Sixty-two was a lot,' he said sympathetically.

I don't think I have ever felt so humiliated or so hollow as I did right then. I didn't cry. I didn't look at Daniel. I felt this pain in my chest and in my throat, a hard pain, like a hot stone. I kept swallowing. It made no difference.

And then, quite ridiculously, all of the cats started to move around. At first they divided into two groups. Then, in their groups they mingled and pushed, and one of them took a swipe at another who ignored him and moved on. I glanced at Daniel, who frowned. Then his mouth opened and he let go of my arm. In the garden, the cats had organised themselves into two groups and had sat down nose to tail. One group had come together to form the shape of a six. The other, the shape of a two.

George looked up at me and nodded. I thought I had better check.

'Do you see that?' I asked Daniel.

'Yes,' he said quietly.

'What do you see?'

'I see the number sixty-two,' he said.

'Can I tell George they can go now?'

He nodded.

I opened the window and said, 'Thank you all very, very much.' I may have been crying, which doesn't impress cats.

'Does he believe you?' asked George.

'George wants to know if you believe me,' I said.

'If you can't talk to cats you have one hell of a variety act,' Daniel said.

'But do you believe me?' I asked.

He nodded and I realised what I had probably known since I was eleven: that being believed was not enough. We had sex that night, but it was different to the last time. This time it felt hesitant. When he touched me, it wasn't like he was exploring my texture, rather that he was feeling to see if I was real. I may have been too self-conscious. I wanted the evening to mean something, but of course everything means something. It's just that you don't always get to choose what that something is.

That was the end of our affair. He never called me and I didn't call him. We managed to never be alone together at work and we certainly behaved as though we had never touched each other. Or shared anything like a secret.

I told myself the things we tell ourselves. That difference is a curse, men scare easily, that I was naïve or deserved better or was foolish. I told myself that no man could love a woman who could talk with cats. But that at least I had tried; tried to squeeze through the gap in the fence and fit myself into the rest of the world, and I had got pushed back out. When it came to relationships I chose not to try again. I am okay with that. Safe and not alone. I have the cats. I have all of the cats.

Burning Buildings, Healing Hands

I AM OLD now. My hearing is poor and the skin on my arms is thin and nearly transparent. I don't talk as much as I used to. I wonder if I used up all my words when I was a teacher, and it was my job to fill rooms and heads with stories about wars and dynasties, and the Industrial Revolution. But in truth, sometimes it hurts a little to talk because I have to breathe more and it makes my chest ache. So I am quiet. And that's okay. But there is a story I need to tell one more time. I realise you will think it is an old man talking nonsense and you may just tell me to rest and you may simply imagine what I say to be dull – or worse, a symptom of my infirmity.

If I tell the nurses, who pop in and mime attention without ever asking a question that isn't either rhetorical or about body functions, that I once walked through a raging fire to rescue screaming children, they would neither listen nor hear. If I persisted and told them that I lifted burning oak beams that blocked our way with my bare hands, with these bony weak hands, or that I had jumped from a second-floor window with a child in each arm and survived, they would think me deluded, ridiculous, a liar. But I need to tell the story. I need to put it into the world one last time. I need to leave it there.

I don't think they can see what preceded this translucent skin. If the good nurses can imagine the good, rich life that constructed this decay, they don't see anything extraordinary within it. At best, they see photographs of my children and grandchildren, and a man who smiles through the humiliation of what they call 'personal care'; who doesn't spit when they talk over him when his genitals are on display. But I did something remarkable once. And I don't tell of it now because I need to be admired. I tell it because small and remarkable things deserve attention and because I like to imagine that if they stay in the world longer than I do then they may become contagious. And, perhaps more selfishly, I am telling this because I need to remind myself that I have lived. That the collection of increasingly vague snapshots that feel as though they were part of someone else's life were real; that I was real and, once at least, I did good things.

It was 1962 and I was twenty-eight years old. I have little sense of the man I was before the fire. My recollection is that I was a bit of a loner, but I remember laughing with friends at teacher-training college, and in the pub, and on the way home from football. I don't remember talking about things and I don't remember feeling very much. I don't think we had to feel as much then as people do now. Or if you did, you didn't have to name whatever it was you were feeling.

I remember smoky staff rooms. I remember curmudgeonly old men who smelt of butterscotch and tobacco and who hated children and who taught maths or woodwork or geography. I remember a young blonde English teacher called Carol. Her eyes glistened when she spoke and she bit her lip when she was listening. On a good day, when I wasn't full of self-doubt, I imagined this was a sign of concentration. On the other days – most days, actually – I assumed she was simply biting herself in order to not drift off because I was so boring. Yet – and I know the memory plays tricks and that the past reorganises itself and some of it fades completely from view – I know I kissed Carol before the fire, at the end of Brighton Pier. We'd gone to see Billy Fury. Great show – Alvin Stardust was on the bill when he was Shane Fenton. We ate warm doughnuts and walked along the seafront talking about music, Carol's sister, who she worried about, and Mr Mason who taught Geography and looked about fifty-five but Carol says was under thirty.

Later, much later, after the fire, Carol and I undressed each other in my bedsit. I remember crying. Not because it was our first time, and not because I didn't know what else to do with love. I was crying because my hands were available to me; because I could move my fingers to undo her blue cotton dress. I could still feel her skin. I never felt luckier than I did in that moment.

I taught History. I loved the subject, still do. It shows us what it is to be human in ways biology and even poetry can't. More, History shows you how you are feeling about the world; how much sympathy you have for it, whose side you are on and how tiny you are. I was never a good judge of smell, certainly not of a chemical smell. And so, while I noticed that the science lab was pungent when I walked past, I didn't think of it as dangerous or even unusual. Science smells, or at least it did in the early 1960s. My mind was on my class – Second Years, you'd call them, Year Eights now. Twelve-year olds. A disquieting mix of babies and bags of burgeoning hormones, faced with me telling them about the rise of Mussolini.

Not that we got beyond the title, me telling them to settle down, me telling them that, yes, I could smell the funny smell but I didn't know what it was and, no, I didn't think it was anything to worry about and, yes, Hitler really admired Mussolini and then there was an enormous explosion, the loudest thing I had ever heard. For a moment there was silence, and then screaming.

My class was on the first floor of what was then considered a modern three-storey building but would now be considered a swollen warehouse with too much glass. Our school was the result of the post-war building programme. We felt modern and safe. The ground floor had a library and offices. We, along with Geography and English, were the next floor up and Science was at the top. I still wonder why they thought Science should be at the top.

I felt the ceiling shake and the large tiles begin to crack and loosen. I heard the quiet that followed the explosion, the inhalation of the children before they screamed. I noticed everything and I can remember the moments now as if I were watching them in slow motion on a grainy, discoloured film.

I am relieved and rather proud to say that I didn't have to persuade myself to instantly do the right thing. Afterwards I wondered what it would have been like if I had felt panic or uncertainty but I didn't. I breathed in and became filled with a clear-headed responsibility for my class. I wanted to go and see what had happened but I pushed that to the side and concentrated my attention on the twenty-eight twelve- and thirteen-year-olds who were staring at me.

'Right,' I said, more loudly than I have ever spoken to a classroom before. 'This is why we have fire drills. Leave your bags, walk in pairs to the stairs. Do. Not. Run. Please, let's make your parents proud of how you do this.' I know I smiled as I said the last bit and I really think that helped.

To their absolute credit they did exactly as I asked and I stood beside the door with the register in my hand and counted them out. When the room was empty, I walked to the top of the stairs and I watched them go down. I followed them out of the building and shouted, 'stay together!' as much to let them know we were all together as to advise them not to break ranks and run for home. When we left the building, everyone looked up. There was smoke coming out of the second-floor windows. There was a little panic then. The children began to spread out from each other, and the outdoors invited running. I remember shouting: 'Come on please, let us finish what we started. Let's get on to the grass together away from this building.' And they listened. Even now I feel a prickling behind my eyes when I remember how they listened. They did so very well that day.

We stood on the playing field next to two other classes and we watched as other groups approached. We watched as the smoke grew thicker and the first flickers of flame appeared from an end window, and I called the names from the register again just to be safe. They were all there. I told them I was proud of them, that they had done well, been responsible, grown-up, that I would tell their parents. As I made my speech, filled with relief and pride and with my eyes drawn constantly to the building I had just left, seven, eight, nine classes and teachers taking registers spread across the playing field. Each class huddled together and all of them, as the smoke grew thicker and the flames more visible, edged backwards, moving further from the fire. As the smoke became darker, we could hear the sirens of the fire engines. It was only then when I – and I assume everyone else staring at the heart of the fire – wondered who had been in that room.

As it turned out it had been First Years, our youngest pupils, the ones in the blazers that looked too big and the eyes that looked as though they might cry if you asked them a question they did not know the answer to. Despite what others might think, I believe that it was to the eternal credit of Science teacher Mr Timothy Witton that he got most of them out. Yes, he smelt of butterscotch and tobacco, no he did not like children, but he would have died before he deserted them. The two children who were not with his class had gone to the toilet before the explosion. He knew that and had to choose instantly between getting the twenty-seven crying eleven- and twelve-year-olds out of the burning building, and telling them to sit still while he went looking for the other two. He did the right thing and he did it when doing the right thing was hard. And I will say this now, and saying it makes my chest hurt, thinking it makes my heart race, he never recovered. Not in his head. Not in his life. I saw him gently beginning to cry as he turned back toward the fire. Mr Witton was a small, stout man who probably looked older than he was, but was old nonetheless. With the same breath I had inhaled after the explosion, I shouted, 'Mr Witton, Mr Witton, would you mind keeping an eye on my lot for a moment?' And I walked very quickly back toward the building.

I don't know what I felt. I don't know what I thought. I saw the fire engine approaching. I didn't think to wait for the professionals. I didn't think anything. I followed my body. I think I heard shouting. I think I heard the headmaster; he may have shouted at me and he may have sworn. I did hear Carol. I could always hear Carol. It must be a strange idea if you look at me now. That these shaking hands and yellow, weak arms thought they were strong; these clouding eyes didn't see the people shouting as these brittle, chicken legs ran into a burning building.

The ground floor was okay. There was a thin smoke that would have scared you if you were on your way to class and a bitter smell of dust and dirt and burning wood but that was all. I ran up the stairs and I thought about my breathing. I thought about it for the first time since I was a child and I had lain on the grass in the back garden and held my breath as a cloud passed over me. As I walked up the stairs, I thought about holding my breath and decided that would be unwise. It would mean deep inhalation and too much gasping. I began to count in my head. I don't know why.

The first floor was thick with smoke and there was a low hum. When I looked up, I just saw black. But I didn't feel heat, not real heat. I felt its promise, though. I kept counting.

The heat came on the second floor. As soon as I touched the top step, I felt it and I saw the heart of the blaze. It was yellow with pockets of blue. Afterwards, when I closed my eyes and saw the fire, I imagined the blue was the flame resting. It pulsed rather than flickered. It waited and it threatened. Despite the heat, it was the smoke that assaulted me. I walked into it and saw nothing and coughed and stopped counting. I crouched down and the smoke was a little thinner and I breathed in slowly, carefully. I realised I had no idea where to go and also that if I walked into the room where the fire was at its most violent, I would not come out. And, of course, I knew that Mr Witton would not have left children in there. I knew that absolutely.

To the left of the science room was a corridor. I edged along the wall and I noticed the paint peeling off and the ceiling creaking. I saw the toilets, although the way to them was blocked by rubble, and two enormous oak beams had fallen and wedged themselves in a criss-cross brace across the door of the girls' toilets. And I knew that the girls were in there. My body moved forward, choosing to ignore the fact that it was impossible to get to them.

My lungs felt as though they were filling up with silt and there were only small pockets of space left at the top of them for air to sit in. The skin on my face was stinging, the top of my head too. I shouted 'Hello' loudly, for fear of not having the breath to do it again and to remind myself I was looking for children and not just catching fire.

I saw the toilet door move slightly – just an inch – and I saw the fingers of a small hand clutch the door, move it the two or three inches it could move before it hit the oak beam and I thought, 'how brave you are to do that. To not curl up in a ball and sob. How very brave.'

I felt the heat in my feet now, like I was walking on hot coals with no shoes. I found out later that the soles of my shoes had melted and moulded themselves to my feet.

I walked toward the door. I didn't run, I walked. I said very clearly, 'are you both in there?' Two thin, teary voices said, 'yes.' Nothing else, just 'yes'.

'Okay,' I said, staring at the oak beams that were at least ten feet long and nearly a foot wide. 'I'll have you out in a jiffy.' I always remember that I used the word 'jiffy'.

I began moving some of the rubbish – the ceiling tiles and plasterboard – out of the way, all the time staring at the beams that formed to make a brace keeping the door closed.

'What are your names?'

'Nancy,' said one.

'Susan,' said the other. You don't get many children called Susan now, do you? Or Nancy, for that matter. My granddaughter is called Ellie. I never taught an Ellie, though I must have taught dozens of Susans. Names come and go, I suppose.

'I'm Mr Styles, you'll have me for History next year,' I said. 'I hope you like History.'

'I like History,' said one of the girls plaintively, as if offering additional incentive to me to get her out.

The thing I remember most about what happened next was that I didn't think. I simply stopped processing what

I was doing or where I was. I certainly did not think about physicality, or myself, or about being human. I simply grabbed the top beam, made a grunting noise (which I remember because smoke came out of my mouth) and I picked it up like it was a garden chair. It moved the way a small kitchen table would have moved and I pushed it away.

I grabbed the other beam, which was wedged in between the door and the opposite wall. It was charred black. It was stuck and too hot to handle but it moved. I gripped it as tightly as I could, gave my hands to the wood, and my imagination tells me I heard a hissing sound which was the skin on my hands burning. I pulled it until it lifted clean off the ground. I don't know if it was an act of God or a rip in the universe but I moved it. I know I moved it because as I opened the toilet door I heard the voice of a fireman at the top of the stairs say, 'Holy Christ, how did you do that?'

I remember grabbing both children and running toward the stairs. I remember one of the children saying, 'your hands are on fire.' And I remember handing one girl – Nancy, as it turned out – to the fireman who said, 'we can't use the stairs.' He pointed to a large window looking out over the playing fields. I could see the kids, the fire engines, Mr Witton. I could see Carol.

'Are we jumping?' I said. I don't remember him saying anything. He put down Nancy and I picked her up. He threw some concrete at the window and it broke. He used his hammer or his axe or whatever it was to smash the glass out of the way. He turned to take Nancy but for some reason I couldn't let either of them out of my sight. All I could think of was getting them to Mr Witton so he could finish his register. So, I jumped with an eleven-year-old under each arm and I landed on my feet so as not to hurt them and I had the sharpest shooting pain through my legs and into my hip.

I'm told I did not let go of the girls until Mr Witton was beside me. I'm told I was smoking like a dying fire after the fireworks had finished. I was lifted onto the grass away from the burning building. All I remember was that I couldn't breathe and I couldn't be sick. I remember people trying to wrap things around me and the fireman who had followed me in and out of the building putting his hands on my shoulder and looking upset. I couldn't lie still. I just wanted to crawl along the floor and put my mouth against the cool damp grass. I felt like I wanted to eat the earth.

I think I wanted to die. I think that all of the pain I had deferred when I was in the building came to me on the grass, and whenever someone tried to touch me Carol says I screamed. My hands felt stripped of skin. My insides were on fire, my feet felt like exposed bloody stumps, my body all charred and soft. My eyes were closed but I imagined I was black like burnt coal; I was spent.

But I need to tell you this. People were surrounding me; I knew because of the noise. They were touching me and I was flinching. Someone was trying to put a mask on me but I was hiding my face in my chest. I was curled up. Susan, the girl I had carried out, had gone to her parents. Parents had seen the fire, heard the fire engines. It was a local school in a small town and people had come. They had hugged each other I imagine. They may have cried. I heard later that Mr Witton cried. Nobody ever mentioned that when he was present for fear it sounded unkind. I think that is strange too.

Susan came back though with her mum and her dad. I heard voices, grown-up voices, but I don't know what they were saying, just that they were busy voices, anxious, disputing, fussing. I heard Susan say, 'I do like History, Mr Styles.'

Carol says that Susan knelt down beside me and I think I remember her whispering something else to me, but I don't know what it was. I just know it felt calm and reassuring. I remember her touching my arm and my body stopped feeling like it was on fire. Then she touched my head with her other hand and I found I could breathe a little. Then, quite quickly, I realised I could breathe a lot.

I opened my eyes and looked up, and saw Susan staring at my hands. Above her stood two adults who I instantly understood to be her parents. They looked at me and the father nodded. The woman, who had blonde hair tied into a plait, knelt down beside her daughter. They looked at each other and simultaneously took one hand each. I was reluctant to unclench my hands; I may have resisted but they overcame my pulling by being gentle. Gentleness is always so very hard to resist.

My hands were badly burnt; the skin was gone, the muscles and tendons wrecked, but as they held my hands, I felt them repair. And I felt my skin growing back. I felt my body come back to me and I began to cough, and kept coughing, violently, until my lungs could fill with air again.

Susan and her mother did not move their hands from me until I stopped coughing. Until my feet stopped bleeding, screaming, aching. Until I knew I would be able to walk barefoot on the grass.

There was something in the paper and I was a local hero for a day or two. I got flowers and Susan's and Nancy's parents bought me a vase with a Phoenix painted on the side. And I carried on teaching History. Susan and Nancy did pass through my class and they both did well – I think they tried extra hard. Nancy did History at university.

And that is my story. I like to think I have hundreds of others because there is no such thing as an ordinary life, but I know everything else I have to tell fades in comparison, or becomes a tiny flake in bigger histories of parliaments and kings and wars.

I know that if the nurse reads this, she will think me mad or foolish or simply absurd. But if she wants to, she can ask Carol when she comes in and Carol will say, 'Yes, it is all true. All of it.' And perhaps one of the nurses will say that it is not unheard of, that people can develop superhuman strength in times of crisis, when they need to save someone or themselves. They'll say people can grow superpowers when they need them and aren't people remarkable. They may even cross themselves because I have noticed that the nurses here do that a lot.

And Carol will smile and say, 'yes, people are remarkable.' And then she will add, because we always, always do, 'it's not just a story about my husband though, is it?'

Tony Saunders and the
Great White Shark

YOU KNOW YOU should be doing something else but you are not quite settling into it. You are easily distracted at the best of times, but today you can't settle and the internet is just a click away. Another picture of a cat playing piano in its pyjamas, that nagging question at the back of your head. Just who did win the League Cup in 1966? And whatever happened to that post-punk band you thought were going to be bigger than U2 but nobody else liked? The thing about the Internet is that it is always available, full of endless stuff, yet never even close to complete. It is laced with half-told stories. It can be quite lazy, can the Internet. Millions of beginnings, not so many endings, a lot of mystery, a lot of half-hearted shrugging. And if one of those billion hints at a story catches your eye, you can spend a ridiculous amount of time in libraries, and writing emails to strangers, trying very hard to find out how it ends. This story is, in some respects at least, a public service. I did it so that you don't have to. I went looking for an ending. I should say now that I wanted it to finish with Steven Spielberg or Peter Benchley standing in the wings watching. If either of them was there, I couldn't see them.

In 1970 Tony Saunders and another Englishman called Richard Buckley were swimming in the blue warm waters that rolled onto a Sydney beach. They had met a couple of days before in a bar and shared their pale English excitement at the heat, the colours, and the prospect of swimming in a massive ocean. They were not stupid and had sought advice on currents and conditions and been reassured by lifeguards who were matter-of-fact about the everyday risks: rip tides, large waves and big fish. All of those things happened but mostly they happened in other places or on other days. Swimming was fine, they said. 'We do it all the time.'

Tony and Richard were testing each other the way men do – who was the strongest swimmer, the quickest, the most comfortable – and as such it is probable that they went out a little further than they might have, and stayed in a little longer too. But they were on holiday, and swimming within their capabilities, and it was Australia so the lifeguard was familiar with excessive testosterone in the water.

It is important to remember that this was 1970, so great white sharks were not located in the consciousness in the way they came to be a few years later. In fact the chances are Tony didn't know about them, which must have made what happened next all the more terrifying.

From the snippets of reports that remain, or at least are findable, the shark came out of nowhere and attacked Richard Buckley from the side. It didn't bite a chunk from his ribs, but rather held him and swam, pushing Richard sideways. Blood left him before flesh did. In fact, it looked as though he had only received puncture wounds while the shark had him in his mouth. It was only when the shark let go that Tony saw Richard's left arm was missing up to the shoulder and the water was cloudy with blood.

Nobody knows what happened next because nobody asked Tony if he tried to help Richard – not that helping Richard was remotely an option – or if he turned and swam for the beach. The sense is that one of those 'it all happened too fast' moments arrived and Tony froze. He probably saw the shark turn and take off Richard's right leg and hip and he definitely saw the shark appear to look at him. He told his daughter that a thousand times. Tony maintains that the shark was over twenty feet long and he swears it swam toward him but went straight past, circling him widely, confidently. Tony turned in the water and watched as the shark began to leave its circle and swim directly at him. He started beating the water, not to scare the shark away so much as to remind himself that he was awake, alive, had some vague and pointless volition available. He did not believe the shark cared and nor did he believe the people on the beach could hear him shouting, nor that they would come into the water even if they did. He beat the water because it felt like the last time he would ever do something, and he didn't want to do nothing.

He saw the shark accelerate as it swam directly at him. He thought about trying to punch it in the eye and he thought about his kids but the shark, again, swam straight past. It took another bite out of the lifeless half body of Richard Buckley and Tony turned and started swimming for shore. He didn't swim fast, not as fast as he could, partly because he didn't imagine for one moment that the shark wasn't going to catch him and partly because it is hard to swim when you are weeping. After what felt like two or three minutes but was probably twenty strokes, Tony stopped and looked back. Sure enough, he could see the giant fin in the water coming toward him. Tony stayed on his back. He vaguely heard some noises from the beach, but they didn't register. He just watched the fin get closer and closer and then dip under the water.

He felt the shark brush his leg and ribs, not with its teeth but with its body. He thought it was playing with him, but sharks don't play. He knew that because he had seen one eat Richard Buckley.

The shark turned again and swam back toward Tony, away from the beach. This time Tony was ready. He was going to try to dodge the shark, which might have made a great name for a board game or a punk band, but was about as rational as Richard Buckley's mother asking, on later being told what had happened, 'Is he dead?'

Tony didn't need to dodge the shark; the shark swam slowly toward him. Tony maintained that it was staring at him the whole time, and then it swam past, flicking Tony's feet with its tail as it did so, and that was the last Tony saw of the shark. It may be that the shark went and ate the rest of Richard; it was certainly the case that no body parts washed up on the shore. Tony swam for the beach where people had gathered. Two lifeguards ran into the water, albeit not very far, and pulled him from the sea. Tony lay on the beach in the recovery position, sand in his eyes, staring at the sea. Looking for the shark. A tiny part of him wanted to lift his arm to wave but he didn't have the strength.

Tony Saunders was a Post Office engineer when there was a Post Office with engineers. He started with them in the mid-60s and was working for them in 1970 when, sadly, his mother died. She left him a lot of nice memories and a house in Solihull that he didn't need. An only child with two young children of his own and a wife called Rita – who worked behind the counter of the local post office and had a beehive haircut some time after other people stopped having them – Tony was settled in a house in Lichfield. He and his family had a nice life and, given these were difficult times for a lot of people, they had the grace to realise their good fortune and the temperament to celebrate it.

Tony had always wanted to travel. When they were dating, he and Rita would talk about visiting California, Hawaii and, when they were feeling most excited, Australia.

So, when Tony sold his mum's house, he did the sensible thing sensible people do with a windfall: he bought tickets for the holiday of a lifetime to Australia.

Australia was even further away in 1970 than it is now and the plane journey felt like torture the children never imagined would end. Tony tried to keep them cheerful, but what was particularly hard for the kids was the knowledge that they would have to endure the journey again on the way back. They could not imagine any holiday being worth it.

Thirty years later, Tony's daughter, Diane, gave an interview to a local paper about her dad and spent most of the time talking about the flight. I wonder if Tony threw himself into the holiday with such astonishing vigour to take the kids' minds off the trip home.

Anyway, Australia was, of course, beautiful. Different smells, different textures, and kangaroos. The people were different too, but you could understand most of what they said and the beaches were like countries in their own right. It was the beaches that Tony loved most.

Tony had always been a keen swimmer, or as keen a swimmer as you can be growing up miles from the sea. He had been into the water every day of the holiday until the shark attack, but had spent the next two days being interviewed by local newspapers and TV about what had happened. The tone of the reporting was very different to the way it might be now. The printed articles are actually quite straightforward reporting. They probably linger over his Englishness a little more than one might expect, seeming to imply that somehow you had to be stupid to swim there given the potential for shark attacks and if the swimmers had been Australian the great white would have stayed away.

The local TV – there is a grainy clip of it on YouTube that was used as part of a 70s documentary on sharks – is quite a stilted affair. Tony, a prematurely balding, fair-skinned man in crimplene trousers and an ironed, checked shirt, stood with his hands behind his back as if reporting to a school headmaster. He gave short answers to clipped questions.

'What happened?'

'What did you think?'

'What did you feel?'

'Have you spoken to Mr Buckley's family?' The only long answer he offered was: 'It looked at me, turned around, and I thought I was going to die but it swam past … right past.'

'You're feeling like a very lucky man?' said the reporter, who was pretty much phoning it in.

And if you pause the interview there for a minute you have, or at least I had, the sense that Tony Saunders had given that pretty obvious observation an awful lot of thought. But he didn't speak. He nodded. And there was silence before the interviewer closed with: 'very lucky indeed'.

In Diane's interview she says that her dad went swimming again two days later. He swam from a different beach, five or six miles down the road. 'The bloody things can move about, you know,' Rita had said.

'They are very territorial actually,' lied Tony, adding, 'and anyway, what are the chances of being struck by lightning twice?' To which Rita replied, 'It's not lightning, it's a bloody big shark, you berk.'

But Tony, who was fast running out of aphorisms and sincerely hoped that the conversation didn't go on much longer, went with, 'It's like falling off a horse. If I don't get straight back on again I never will.'

In truth, something profound had happened for Tony the moment the shark's tail brushed past his leg. He felt something, something between him and the shark. It was something wordless, and so something that had to remain private. In fact, it wasn't simply beyond explaining, it was beyond understanding. It resembled a communion, a peace. It felt like transcendence.

Tony wasn't getting back in the water assuming that the shark would never come near him again. He was getting back into the water expecting that it would.

Tony went swimming every day for the next week. The local paper did a little follow-up story on him on the day of Richard's funeral. It presented him as stoical, stubborn, perhaps eccentric (there was little chance they could describe an Englishman as brave), and hinted that he was perhaps honouring his 'friend' by swimming for him.

Tony came face to face with a great white shark again two days after Richard Buckley's funeral. If nobody had been there to see it nobody would have noticed it, and this tiny fragment of a story would not exist. But a small fishing boat had seen a great white and had followed it for about fifteen minutes. They saw Tony in the water and they shouted and waved their hands. He waved back and he heard the words 'shark' and 'get out of the water' but he pretended he didn't. Instead he kept on swimming parallel with the beach. He saw the shark fin from about fifty feet away. When it got to within twenty feet he stopped dead and dived under the surface. The shark accelerated towards him and Tony's nerve went. He bobbed to the surface, gasped for one last mouthful of air before he was ripped in two, but the shark did not bite him. It swam past, less gently than last time. It bumped into him quite hard, bruising his ribs. Tony felt it was chastising him, telling him not to take advantage, not to test, not to belittle what had been agreed between them. Tony felt the urge to say sorry to the shark. Instead he rolled on to his back and kicked gently toward the beach. It felt like acknowledgement. He was sure the shark would understand.

He contemplated not telling Rita but unfortunately that was not an option. The fishermen insisted on buying him a beer and on finding out that he was the bloke who survived the attack the previous week they told everyone what they had seen. The more beers they had, the more dramatic the story. By the time the press were informed Tony had been labelled 'The English Shark Whisperer', which pleased him and worried him at the same time. He was pleased that his unique relationship had been noticed, named and respected. He was worried – and he knew how ludicrous this was – that the sharks would find out and think he was trying to cash in on his ... what was it? Gift? Power? Union?

This made him coy. He was feeling strange things, things that unsettled him, and Tony was an ordinary man. Unusual things were not welcome in his world. The extraordinary had no currency at the Post Office. There were people who thought he had got above himself for getting himself a passport. Making friends with twenty-foot sharks was blatantly showing off.

Anyway, as far as one can tell Tony was quietened by the second shark experience. Rita suggested he might want to swim in a pool for a while and so he did, although he didn't enjoy it in the same way.

Tony disappears for over a year then. In 1971 there is an archive of him being interviewed, quite half-heartedly it seems, for a local Midlands paper that, for no apparent reason, did a random piece on what it was like to survive a shark attack. It's fair to say the article is thin on quotes and I can imagine Tony trying very hard to impress upon the reporter that he was not attacked, that he was present when someone else was attacked and later he was simply present, but the shark, or sharks, (Tony maintained that it was two different sharks with two different temperaments) did not attack him. The article was really more interested in the carnage that befell Richard Buckley than the sparing of Tony Saunders. There is a picture of Tony though, looking a tiny bit tubbier than the YouTube clip and to my eyes slightly more irritable or at least less patient.

We know now that great white sharks cannot be held in captivity. The longest a great white has been kept is forty-four days. The second longest is sixteen days. They don't like it. They get depressed. They stop eating or if you put them with other fish they eat them, then they get depressed. They smash their heads against the glass and wait to die. They crave the ocean, they need the space. We know this now, of course, but in 1971 we knew an awful lot less, and frankly we didn't really care all that much. But there was some curiosity, some interaction. It came in the form of a great white shark cage, which had existed since 1965. And it was back in Australia.

Craig Mensall had miraculously survived a horrific attack by a great white in 1963. To this day he has part of a shark's tooth embedded in his wrist. His diaphragm was punctured, his lung ripped open, his abdominal cavity fully exposed and all of his ribs on his left-hand side were broken. He needed 423 stitches. He wrote about the attack and his recovery, which involved overcoming his fear of water. He had been a champion surfer and was defending his championship when he was attacked. It was his attempts to overcome his fear, to make his way back to the sea, that led him to build the first shark cage.

Tony was fascinated by Mensall, by his survival, his whole experience. He wanted to know what affinity Mensall had with the shark, if Mensall felt some of the things Tony felt. And it is possible that Tony felt something else too, something unspeakably smug, because he had met two sharks and collected no teeth and no stitches.

Tony's desire to go back to Australia became overwhelming. He and Rita separated for five months in early 1972; one suspects that the drive to return across the world to dive with sharks might have had something to do with that. Regardless of how one imagines the experience of being beside a great white when it has a mouth full of your friend, it will probably change you profoundly, no matter how you decide to embed it into your life.

In late 1972, in an apparent attempt to cement their reconciliation, or so their daughter Diane says, Tony and Rita went back to Australia. It was, in a way the previous trip had never quite been, the holiday of a lifetime. They went to Ayers Rock, camped in the outback, visited Sydney Opera House and saw Led Zeppelin play, which they would not have thought about doing if they had toured Birmingham.

And Tony met Craig Mensall. Mensall described a quiet, nervous Englishman who seemed shy. He did not ask Mensall about his attack but Tony did, with some reticence at first, tell him of the attack that killed Richard Buckley and of his other encounter with the second shark.

'It was probably the same shark,' Mensall told him. 'They are solitary creatures.'

Tony was unconvinced but was too embarrassed to say so. He knew that Mensall was an expert and that the vague impressions of a Post Office engineer who lives as far from the sea as you can on a small island – a sea, incidentally, that had as many great white sharks as it had mermaids – would seem foolish. But not saying what you believe does not make the belief go away, or the feelings that accompany it and Mensall, a generous and thoughtful man, asked Tony if he would like to go down in the cage. Tony said yes very quickly, despite the fact he had never used scuba gear in his life.

Craig Mensall wrote a little about what happened with Tony in the cage. He described Tony as calm and concentrated. Not afraid. He told him that often they go down and no sharks come and to expect to be disappointed. 'They'll come,' said Tony. 'They'll come for me.' Adding, 'assuming they can recognise me under all this gear.' Mensall laughed. Tony didn't.

But come they did. Mensall is not expansive but he is generous, reflecting, 'The sharks did come, a little quicker than usual, and Mr Saunders, despite being told very clearly not to do this, reached his arm through the cage as the great white swam past, patting it like a horse. It was rash and stupid, not something I would expect from someone who had seen what he had seen. The great white did stay a little longer than usual perhaps. I wouldn't look to make meaning from that personally.'

Tony probably did. His daughter said the only time she ever heard he had cried was after he had been down in the cage. 'Mum thought it was because he was being reminded of the horror of the attack, but the tears she described came from somewhere else, I always thought. I could be wrong. We often were where dad was concerned.'

Tony and Rita were due to leave three days after Tony had been down in the cage. The last part of the holiday was spent as it was planned; lazing around near Sydney, window-shopping, sunbathing, looking for something nice to take home for the kids.

The day before they were due to go home Tony said he wanted one last swim. He laughed at himself as he said that he would stay close to shore, not be silly and absolutely not wander off with any great white strangers. Rita was reassured by his tone. It had been a good holiday, it felt to her as though something was ending. Perhaps Tony's preoccupation was fading. The word 'resolve' was not used as often in 1972 as it perhaps is now, but if it had been Rita might have used it.

Tony never came back. He went to the beach nearest the hotel but walked along the sand and road for nearly three miles until he got to the part of the beach he had swum from with Richard Buckley. The lifeguard said 'G'day' and Tony nodded and waved but he didn't take his eyes from the sea. 'Stay within eyesight,' said the lifeguard.

'Of course,' muttered Tony although even then his eyes were fixed some way off shore. Tony barely noticed the first few dozen strokes. He could feel his spine stretch as he reached forward to grab the water and he could feel his toes pointing back toward the beach, waving.

He quite consciously turned to the left to swim along the line of the beach, to be seen by the lifeguard, to be parallel and compliant, but if parallel was like swimming toward nine on a giant clock he was swimming toward 9:30, and then 10, and then 10:30. Tony felt he was heading toward the patch of water that Richard had been taken in. He couldn't be sure it was exactly the same but if he was close enough he felt the shark would find him. For Tony, the shark had told him as much when he lingered beside the cumbersome and unnecessary cage. 'You don't need this silliness,' he seemed to say. 'Metal cages are beneath the likes of you and I.'

It was an hour before the lifeguard gave any serious thought to the clothes on the beach or where their owner might be. He spent five minutes scanning the sea with his binoculars before he notified the beach office and they notified the small boats. Thirty minutes later all boats in the area received a call to be on the lookout for a balding swimmer who may have caught a rip tide, or a current. Police searched the coastline in case he had come ashore further along the beach. Tony had not given thought to who would be looking for him or even why. He had turned from 10:30 to 11:00 and then to 12:00 and then to 1:00 and he had not once looked back. He had felt the change in the water, it had become warmer and then colder and the swell had grown across the reef. He had seen many fish and one or two shadows but no great white shark, not yet.

But he had no doubt it would come, and the sea felt so good it was easy for him to be patient, and he felt so alive in the water that he believed he could swim forever.

Cloaked

A S A CHILD, Anthony had worn bright, clashing colours and socks that didn't match. By ten years, he was beginning to gather self-consciousness in his choices – though he maintained a taste for lime green and raspberry red and his ever-odd socks. By the time he was twelve he had withdrawn into muted pastels and quieter shades the way evening retreats into night.

As a young man, Anthony tended toward clarity of purpose and seeking out order. He realised early – in a woodwork class aged fourteen to be precise – that he enjoyed life more when he knew why he was doing whatever it was he was doing. He was, at the time, making a simple and small bedside table. It didn't require dovetail joints, being held together (much to the disgust of the woodwork teacher) with dowels and screws. He knew that when it was finished, he would take it to his bedside and put things on it. He smiled while he sanded. Nobody noticed.

Despite tending toward the corporeal he believed in God. In fact he believed in quite a classical and traditional God who had a beard but no trousers, who watched the world without getting overly involved in it but who reserved the right to make notes and punish people for wrongdoing when the time came. That time usually being death. It was not a belief he ever questioned. It flowed in him like blood. And he believed, without ever really articulating why or how, in things like avoiding doing harm to others and coming together with your fellow man in the pursuit of a common purpose, as long as that purpose was linked quite directly to some greater good. He liked teams, motifs and group projects. And so it was no surprise that he joined the Army when he was seventeen and he served, as a nurse, for twenty-five years. Anthony married Gwynn when he was twenty-four. Gwynn was very happy to leave home where she had shared a childhood with an older brother who put slugs in her breakfast bowl when he was six and set fire to the family cat when he was thirteen. When she was with Anthony she could breathe. He made her feel relief. After their first date Anthony went home and cried, for want of a better way of pouring his feelings of being completely overwhelmed into the world. Gwynn had a round, pale face with skin that looked softer than air. Others might have considered her plain with a tendency toward a resting expression of disappointment. Anthony believed her to be the most beautiful thing in the world.

They had two children, Matthew and Henry. Gwynn was a teaching assistant. She worked with children who had special needs. She liked it even though she didn't get paid very much. They went on package holidays to a different country every year and had a map in the kitchen upon which they marked each country with a sticker with the year of their visit on it. Anthony kept a notebook in which he wrote something about the holiday, and the marks out of ten everyone in the family had given the country. He was disappointed that even though the past three years had seen them visit Cuba, Iceland and Florida, the marks had got lower each year. This also meant he spent more time planning the next holiday, determined to at least match the eight everyone had given Majorca seven years ago.

On his fiftieth birthday he asked his wife if he had changed. She said that he was 'of course quieter'. In fact, he had grown quieter by the year since they had married, she added. 'I suppose that's what everyone does.'

Anthony couldn't help but feel she said this with a hint of sadness.

Anthony was a diminutive man with a receding chin and a slight paunch that seemed to anchor him to the ground. He worked in education now, teaching nurses how to be efficient and helpful. He liked it, it made him feel useful. In fact, it secretly made him feel like he was doing good. He kept this feeling secret because he thought it was a stupid thing to feel, given the vicarious nature of the good he thought he was doing.

But Anthony, who would have been the first to say that he had everything in the world that he had ever wanted, was beginning to notice that he had a problem; he seemed to be fading from view. It wasn't that he shrunk, more that he became less apparent. He faded into places like water fades into sand.

And this problem was becoming more noticeable as time passed. One day he walked into a classroom and instead of announcing that he was ready to start he just stood and waited for the group of thirty or so students to settle.

But they didn't. Anthony sat on the edge of the desk at the front of the class and waited and smiled, but nothing happened. Perhaps, he reasoned, they were waiting for him to tell them he was ready. Perhaps they thought he was conducting an observation exercise and would tell them something about themselves when he started. Students like to be told about themselves, this he knew. Still, and he liked this about himself, he resisted the urge to speak.

After fifteen minutes one of the students said loudly, 'Perhaps nobody is coming?'

To that Anthony mumbled, 'Hello.'

One of the students stood up. 'I'll go to the office and ask,' she said.

'Hello,' said Anthony more loudly.

The student left.

Anthony thought for a moment. He picked up his bag and left the room. He stood outside breathing deeply and feeling something like fear flushing through him. He re-entered the room and said 'Hello!' as loudly as he could.

'Someone has just gone to look for you,' one of the students said.

'I'm here,' said Anthony. Relieved. Afraid.

And everyone settled.

When he got home, Anthony did not tell his wife. He was afraid that it would disappoint her. Anyway, she was watching cooking programmes on television with Henry. He wasn't entirely sure they knew he was home.

He sat in the kitchen and watched Chelsea play Juventus on the small TV. His son Matthew, who was eighteen and about to go to university to study History, came in, watched fifteen minutes of the game, and shouted to his mum, 'Where's Dad?'

Anthony swore. Nobody seemed to hear.

After the incident in the classroom Anthony began to notice his perceived absence more and more. He noticed that if he was with someone in a lift and a colleague got in, that colleague said hello to the person he was with but not to Anthony.

He noticed he had been missed off a list of staff awaiting a computer upgrade, and on entering his open-plan office heard someone standing over his work station asking: 'Who sits here?' The person he had been sitting next to for four years – her name was Janice, and she had cried on his shoulder when her husband left her for her sister in the run-up to Xmas 2009 and who had bought him a Terry's Chocolate Orange as a thank you – shrugged and murmured: 'Not sure.'

He finally realised that he had vanished when he found himself alone in the lift coming down from the fifth floor at the end of the working day and the head of school, Michelle Fisher – a fifty-something career woman with immaculate blonde hair and perpetually pursed lips – stopped the lift on the third floor, got in, stopped the lift again between floors by pressing the emergency button and got undressed. She removed her brown two-piece business suit and black tights and put on a summer frock. Her underwear didn't match. She wore a red bra and white pants. Anthony didn't want to know that. She had not noticed Anthony standing in the lift. It was a small lift.

Driving home he noticed he was alarmed and underneath that he was sad. And underneath the sadness, he was angry. He had set out to serve the common good and his efforts and his service were unseen. Is that the same as it being unvalued, he wondered? Or worse, of no consequence? And in wondering he noticed that underneath the anger there may have been some self-pity.

Anthony's instinct was to work harder to be seen. That was the appropriate response to a challenge, to try harder. Yet – and this felt courageous to Anthony – he paused before throwing himself at the world. Instead he decided to explore his invisibility, see how far it extended.

He noticed that three colleagues in his open-plan office went for coffee and didn't ask him. Indeed, didn't see him. Later, he heard one of the secretaries call out from behind him: 'Does anyone know where Anthony is?' and the person sitting two desks down didn't even look up before shouting: 'No, not seen him.' And instead of saying anything Anthony stayed quiet. Nervous, confused, not a little cross, but quiet.

In the middle of one afternoon he noticed Vanessa Goldcroft, who was the deputy head of school, arrive for a meeting in Michelle Fisher's office. Vanessa was a short, grey-haired, portly woman who walked as though she was dragging timber on a chain behind her. She hovered outside the office, hesitating and looking around self-consciously. Anthony noticed that he felt a wave of sympathy for her for the way she was standing and waiting without anyone to talk to, and so he instinctively stood up and walked toward her, hoping to catch her eye. He didn't. She didn't seem to see him and so he pretended that he was not walking toward her but was instead walking past her, to the photocopier, or the toilet or oblivion.

Anthony assumed Vanessa was waiting for Michelle because she was on the phone, but as he walked past the door, he saw she was deep in conversation with a sharp-nosed man with shiny black hair and an expensive-looking dark grey suit. As Anthony passed the door Michelle looked up, saw Vanessa and said, 'Come in.' Vanessa smiled and nodded and went in. To Anthony's astonishment, he found himself following her.

Michelle's office was quite large. At one end was her desk, made of proper wood and with a large bay window behind it. In the middle was a round table with six chairs, for meetings and hosting her daily visitors and, running up the side of the office, there was a three-seater burgundy-coloured sofa. It had metal legs and two scatter cushions at either end. Anthony did not imagine people sat on it often but it softened the room, lent it perspective, gave the impression that sometimes people came in and just chatted.

So, Anthony sat on it, being careful not to move any of the carefully positioned cushions.

Anthony noticed that the sharp-nosed man seemed quite comfortable and also that his hair wasn't so much greasy as attended to – that is to say, it had products on it and it was meant to look like that. He was confident. He clearly had not noticed Anthony. In fact, he barely noticed Vanessa.

Michelle introduced him without looking up from the large spreadsheets she was shuffling. 'Vanessa, this is Jeremy Clarke. He is an auditor, here to help us organise our expenditure in a way that is commensurate with the university's financial plan.'

Jeremy nodded at Vanessa. Vanessa nodded back and then realised that Michelle was not telling him her name and so she said, 'Hello, I'm Vanessa Goldcroft.' She paused, perhaps wondering if the next part was necessary or still accurate before deciding that it was required. 'I'm the deputy head of school.'

Nobody saw Anthony, which fascinated him and made him sad at the same time. He had been sitting perfectly still in case they were attracted to movement, but after a few minutes the fear of being unseen outgrew the fear of being caught, so he reached down and scratched his leg. Nothing. Then he scratched his face. Still nothing. He stood up, turned around and sat back down again. Nothing. Michelle, Vanessa, and Jeremy were hovering around the table looking at papers and shuffling notes.

'So,' started Michelle, 'this is not a pleasurable task, but it is a necessary one. I believe we all know that we are overspending. We have been told that we are going to have to make some cuts and Jeremy here is going to help us to do that as painlessly as possible.' She didn't look up as she spoke and nor did she sound convinced.

People use long sentences when they are in important meetings, thought Anthony. Mostly people use short sentences in real life. They hurry because they know someone else is going to want to speak and it is polite to not use up too much space. In meetings they think it is good to take up space. Michelle was still talking. She had the look of a woman whose heart was not in her words, words that seemed to be surrounding her.

'One would like to think we can do this sensitively but we also need to be aware that this is a business and staff are assets or in some cases…' She trailed off and looked at Jeremy.

'In some cases not,' he finished.

Anthony was looking at his own shoes. It felt terribly intrusive to be listening to a conversation about people he worked with, rude even. And so he instinctively looked at his feet and decided to give them some long-overdue attention. He remained instinctively polite, even when he was trespassing in his boss' office. Realising the absurdity of this contradiction, Anthony put his hands in his pockets, drew his legs in and leant forward like a student trying to appear interested, deciding that he should pay attention.

Michelle Fisher, with Jeremy Clarke's encouragement, was listing names of people who were, in their view, disposable. They only said names, and as they did so Vanessa winced slightly but, perhaps mindful of her senior position – a position that required her to attend to the needs of the people who were above her in the chain of command rather than the people below her – she said nothing. As the names were mentioned, Anthony noticed that despite his less-than-low profile he knew a little something about all of them. He couldn't remember how he knew, but he knew nonetheless.

Jenny was a quiet young teacher who liked rowing and who had asked Anthony questions about his children when they first met five or six years ago. She remembered his answers a year later when they were sheltering from rain in the school foyer. Ben was a young mental health lecturer with astonishingly good teeth. He liked music very much but once missed a concert by his favourite band because he had found Jenny crying at her desk at six in the evening because she had not been selected for the Olympic rowing trials. He did not tell her about the gig. Anthony thought that was kind.

Lucy was nearly sixty. Single, quirky, difficult. Needy. She complained a lot and irritated people because she was pious and smelt of pencils. Anthony knew she lived with her mother who had dementia and was incontinent and liked to draw all the time. They were all going to lose their jobs.

As was Gemma, a thin nervous woman who cried at the graduation ceremony every year. Then there was Tom who came out when he was forty-two and had his ear pierced to celebrate, only for it to become infected and for his mother to tell him that that was God punishing him. And Eileen – four children, no partner, arms the size of two small ponies, always smiling. She had exhausted eyes. And Anthony. Anthony's name was there. Nobody listed the things he did out loud, but Michelle did say very quietly, 'We hardly ever see him anyway.'

Finally, the list seemed complete and Vanessa summoned up whatever courage she could to say, 'It feels almost random, doesn't it?' And seeing the look on the faces of Michelle and Jeremy she added, 'I mean in some respects this process shows us how disposable we, most of us, are?'

Michelle seemed weary. 'Yes,' she sighed. The three of them sat quietly for a moment looking at the table, the women noticing what they had done, the man wondering when it would be appropriate to leave. Anthony meanwhile thought about getting up and leaving first, unable to bear the idea that they would have to walk past him to get out. But he stayed where he was, drawing his feet in even further so as not to trip anyone up.

Jeremy stood up first. 'Thank you for your time,' he said. 'I will leave it in your capable hands, Professor Fisher. The procedure, I believe, is that you send your list to Human Resources who will in turn send notices of intent to the staff mentioned and invite them to interview to discuss their options, which are of course limited, but it is important to observe appropriate process. I will tell the vice chancellor that reasonable measures have been put into place in a very professional manner, and one hopes that the next time we meet it will be to discuss recruitment or expansion strategies, although one is always mindful of...'

Long sentences again, thought Anthony. Why did he stand up to say all that? Anthony heard himself mutter 'blah blah blah' and Jeremy paused for a moment. Anthony's chest tightened. Speaking was a mistake. Not being seen is one thing, but not being heard?

'...the particular financial challenges the education sector faces.' Jeremy finished what he was saying and nodded.

'Thank you for your help,' said Michelle.

'Sector is a funny word,' thought Anthony.

Vanessa went to say something, and Anthony wondered what it could possibly have been. 'Nice to meet you'? 'Yes, thank you'? 'Goodbye, you soulless bastard'? She raised her hand as if to wave but instead did nothing, putting her hand back into her lap. She looked at Michelle who did not look back at her, and she got up and left, failing to notice Anthony on the sofa as she nearly brushed against his knees on her way out.

Anthony and Michelle were alone in her office now. She sighed as she picked up the staff lists, went to her desk, and shook her computer into life. Anthony watched as she copied the names of those being made redundant into a document and, he presumed, an email.

Her mobile phone rang. She looked at it before answering and smiled. 'I need a drink,' she said when she answered.

There was a pause as the person on the phone replied. Michelle's shoulders relaxed and she raised her eyebrows.

'Yes, that might help too. I'll need to be back in an hour, maybe two.'

She ended the call, stood up, and left her office without looking at the computer screen again. Anthony was left on his own on the sofa, staring at the walls and wondering what his redundancy package might be like.

He stood up and wandered over to Michelle's desk. He thought about sitting down in her chair, but the idea of being seen sitting there by anyone coming in mortified him. He imagined sitting there and Michelle coming back, not noticing him, sitting on his lap. That would be embarrassing. He looked at the computer. The email to Human Resources was open on the desktop. It was neither signed nor sent. He shook his head. It was a shame, he thought. These were nice people. There were less nice people who ought to lose their jobs, or quite nice people for whom losing their jobs might be a blessing. 'Why doesn't being nice ever count for anything these days?' he thought. He stared at his own name on the list.

'I could do this better,' thought Anthony even though he couldn't remember thinking that about anything before in his life. 'I could,' he said out loud, as if to reassure himself. He looked at the handwritten list that had emerged from the meeting. He swallowed hard and he chose not to think about the consequences of his actions, which he noticed was quite an exciting position to take. He screwed up the list and put it in his pocket.

He very tentatively sat down at the desk and deleted all of the names in the email. He took a deep breath, wiggled his fingers and began to type.

Patricia Bethany Fillimore was first on the list because she had too many names and once referred to students as cattle. Bob was next on because he told a sexist joke to some students once and berated them for not laughing. Granted, he had just recovered from cancer but frankly redundancy would be a blessing. He shouldn't be working the hours he did without a bowel.

Liz Booth smelt of lemons and had been here since the late seventeenth century, thought Anthony. She had the IT skills of a stick. She had once emailed the whole university her grandson's Christmas list in the form of a letter to Santa.

Rachel went on because she was a racist. Louise could go because she said 'actually' all the bloody time. Heather Flynn laughed at people instead of with them, and when she did so sounded like a puppy left out in the rain. And Alan Gould could go because he wore a blazer and, on special occasions, a yachting cap.

Anthony was sweating. He noticed he was breathing hard too, and that his left hand was making a child's fist, squeezing his thumb tightly, making the end of his fingers red. 'Who do you think you are, young man,' said Anthony, feigning his mother's voice. 'Nobody,' he heard himself say. 'I am nobody.' But he didn't hover the cursor over the send-button for very long. Rather he looked at it for a moment, took a breath, and clicked.

He was back at his desk, unseen, when Michelle came back. Her cheeks were red. He wondered whether she appeared slightly off balance as she pushed against her office door. It had been a difficult day, he acknowledged. She had been put in a difficult position and that would unsettle anyone. Or, he thought, she might be a bit drunk.

Anthony did not go straight home. He went shopping instead. He bought two new shirts, one of which bordered on purple. The other was checked and came in as subtle a yellow as one could imagine.

When he got home he showed Gwynn. 'I don't remember seeing you in purple before,' she said. 'It's not really purple,' he said quietly. 'It is, Dad,' said Matthew as he stared at the television. 'Not in a Prince sort of way, but it is purple. It's alright.' Anthony didn't say anything. 'Alright' constituted praise, he knew this. He felt a little prickle behind his eyes and swallowed hard.

He didn't sleep very well that night. All he could think was that where there would have been redundancy now there was the sack. At three in the morning, when all he could imagine were the bad things that gathered in his skin he found himself wondering, darkly, rationally, about life insurance and about how being invisible might be a helpful step toward a noble and repentant absence. He wanted to be a good dad, a good husband. And in some ways he had done well. His family were cared for, they had choices in their lives; possibilities. If he could help provide that while he was invisible he could surely continue to offer it when he was dead?

Three days later and it was Friday. He was at his desk early. He had watched as one or two people arrived. Jenny the rower, Ben with the teeth. Anthony was mainly waiting for the blame, still unseen, when Louise stormed in with a brown envelope. Looking around she saw nobody.

'Typical,' she said out loud. 'I cannot actually believe this. Does anyone else have one of these?' She waved her envelope above her head. Nobody spoke. 'Actually, this is bullying,' she said. 'Actual bullying.'

She went out again. A moment later Liz came in looking very pale. She was with Bob. They both had brown envelopes. Ben and Jenny realised that sympathy was required. The four came together in the middle of the large open-plan office and Bob said the words 'redundancy'.

'Early retirement,' said Liz proudly. 'It's not redundancy, it is early retirement.'

'Not that early in your case, Liz,' said Bob, reminding Anthony why he had put him on the list.

'I'm so sorry,' said Jenny.

'Me too,' said Ben.

'And me,' said Anthony, adding, 'What will you do?'

'Talk to the union I suppose,' said Bob. 'Although it sort of depends on what the deal is.'

Other staff began to arrive, some with envelopes, some without.

'I don't see any black people with a brown envelope,' said Rachel, quietly.

And so it continued. Alan said he simply didn't care. 'More time on the boat. I'm getting too old for this game anyway. It's changed.'

'It has changed,' said Liz. 'I miss the discipline, the dedication, the starch.'

Anthony noticed several things over the next few hours. For one thing, there was no crying. Well, Jenny the rower had a bit of a weep on Ben's shoulder but that happened most weeks and didn't seem directly linked to the fact that they were not losing their jobs. That aside, there was no profound distress. There was some shouting.

Alan did march into Michelle's office and said that he felt this was a bad show, that staff could have been consulted at an earlier point and that he felt this had come out of the blue. Michelle, to her credit, hid her surprise that he had been made redundant very well and quietly said that she was just one part of a detailed audit process that had led to the university making the incredibly difficult decisions it had made – decisions that were as much based on skill mix and the future directions and challenges facing the department as they were on the financial challenges all universities were currently facing.

Vanessa Goldcroft was approached and asked if she had known of the redundancies. As she was approached by Liz, who had not been on the list when she left the office, she could quite honestly say that she was as surprised as anyone else. Anthony saw her go into Michelle's office. He decided to follow her to see what was said but was astonished to find that as he got to the door both women turned and looked at him.

He blushed and to his credit managed to stutter, 'I'm sorry, I was hoping to catch Vanessa. It can wait. Sorry.' And he walked away quickly. He left the main office and stood for a moment outside the lift. He needed air. When the lift door opened Lucy got out. As Anthony passed her to get into the lift he noticed the faint smell of urine. He turned to see her facing him. 'Nice shirt,' she said.

He pulled at his shirt and smiled. 'Thank you,' he said. And as the lift doors closed, he found himself feeling pleased that he had saved her job.

Later in the day Vanessa came and found him. 'You wanted to see me?' she said.

Mostly Anthony was surprised she had remembered. He appeared to no longer be invisible. He was not even forgettable. He felt a little sick – it may have been relief. However, he did not have time to decide what the feeling was because Vanessa was looking at him and he hadn't wanted to see her and he had nothing to say, so he said something honest instead.

'It doesn't matter,' he said. 'It's been a difficult day. It must have been very hard for you too.'

'Why?' she asked, quite softly.

'Because I imagine you must have been part of the series of meetings…'

'Well, I thought I was.' She blushed slightly, perhaps remembering that Anthony was on the list of redundancies that she had expected to go to HR. 'But everything changed after I was involved. Everything.'

'Must have been a difficult process for Michelle then.' Anthony was trying to sound empathetic. He thought it came out a little robotically, but Vanessa didn't seem to notice.

'Yes,' she said, 'although she seems a little surprised herself.'

Anthony was the last person left in the office that night. He didn't need to be there, but he still imagined that he would be in trouble and he preferred that the trouble began here rather than by a phone call to him at home. He had spent the day imagining the police arriving, expecting fingerprints to be taken, witnesses sought. He imagined Jeremy Clarke being asked if there was anyone else who had had access to the content of the redundancy meeting and remembering hearing something, maybe seeing something, remembering Anthony.

When he had first heard his name added to the list of people to lose their jobs, he had quietly decided that he would just carry on coming in to work. After all, nobody would see him, and his pay-off would allow him to trick his family into believing he had a job, for a while at least. He would still come here, and nobody would notice and then later, when he was dead, he would bloody well haunt the place even though still nobody would notice.

But now he was not invisible. Something had drawn him into the light. When they found out and he was blamed, sacked, humiliated, probably sent to prison, he wouldn't be able to come back. He wouldn't be able to hide here anymore. He wouldn't be able to pay his mortgage or support his family.

Anthony noticed, in the fading light of an empty open-plan office, that he was crying like a child. He took some deep breaths. He told himself that this was not professional. He gathered himself in and thought about his Army days. That always made him feel a little bit thinner, a little bit stronger and a lot more contained. He sat up straighter in his chair, breathed deeply, and dried his eyes. He stood up, put his diary, which he had not opened all day, into his otherwise empty bag and walked out of the office.

Anthony pressed the button for the lift and waited. Michelle Fisher appeared beside him. They stood in silence and Anthony prayed that she was not going to take her clothes off. As the lift doors opened, Michelle said quietly, 'Long day.'

Anthony nodded. 'This must be hard for you,' he said.

'Yes, I suppose so.'

'Someone has to do it,' he said meekly.

'It's a process. I make some suggestions but they are only suggestions. Other people discuss things, discussions I am not part of, and the system does the rest. It probably shouldn't be like that but…' She shrugged.

'Yes,' thought Anthony, 'it's the system.'

Michelle added, 'It is what I am paid for, I suppose.'

'I hope you have a nice evening,' said Anthony as softly as he could.

'Thank you,' she said. 'You too, Anthony. And thank you, thank you for noticing that this is hard for all of us.'

At dinner Anthony told his family about the redundancies. 'I feel quite lucky,' he said. 'It could very easily have been me.'

'Nah, Dad,' said Henry. 'The place would fall down if you weren't there.'

'I'm not sure that's true,' he said quietly.

'They value you,' said Gwynn. 'You are dependable, that still counts for something.'

They ate in silence before Anthony said, 'Do you think we should try something different with our holiday this year?'

Negotiating with Angels

I'M A FOOL. I know that now and I'm embarrassed. If I ever meet God, the first thing I am going to do is apologise. Although I suspect he gets that a lot.

It happened in a second-hand shop. Like a lot of second-hand shops, it called itself an Antiques Emporium. It was dusty, charmingly chaotic, and full of old and beautifully useless things – from worn-out furniture to pictures of other people's relatives. I used to love going into shops like that and rooting around. In truth it was something of a hobby and, until I had no strength left, one of my main pleasures.

After I got the diagnosis I found myself visiting more and more second-hand shops. I planned my days around where I could wander to, what sort of odd, outdated, or ridiculous things I could look at and touch. When I was able, I would get the train to somewhere new and prepare an itinerary that took in all of the old second-hand book or antique shops I could find online. When that proved beyond me, I reduced my range.

Second-hand shops are full of second-hand air and I came to feel as though it suited me. It was like matching furniture to the colour of the walls. My lungs were dark and lumpy and when I lay in bed at night and imagined the oxygen reluctantly entering me I pictured it a different colour when it left and I imagined its relief. And even though I was quite young, thirty-seven, I felt old and it seemed appropriate that I should be surrounded by old things; particularly things that had managed to accumulate years more effectively than I had.

I also think that when you have what I have, and you get weaker and thinner and more tired and you slow down and find yourself noticing more because you have to; because you are not in a position to rush on to the next shiny event or person or thing, well then shops with old things in them are a good place to be. Nobody moves quickly in an antiques shop; people meander, and it is a relief not to feel as though you are holding everyone up.

Jenny and I used to come to these places together, but unlike me she always had to buy something. I don't have a problem coming into a shop, walking around, looking at yellowing paperbacks, phallic glass ornaments or broken musical instruments and moving on. Jenny felt good shops required honouring and when I would complain she would say, 'Think of it as an entrance fee.'

Personally, I thought simply being there acted a bit like an entrance fee. When I was a student, I got a part-time job pretending to be engaged. My then girlfriend and I would stand outside jewellery shops in Hatton Garden pointing at rings and occasionally kissing like a cliché. Then we would go in and ask to see some rings. They would only show us the rubbish ones because we were not proper customers. We were hired to attract customers which I thought absurd. The idea that a couple of twenty-year-olds standing outside a jewellery shop would persuade casual passers-by to propose to each other and instantly buy the ring was ridiculous. Yet it worked. People would come and, when there were enough customers, we would quietly leave the shop and move on to the next one or buy coffee. People being in shops attract other people apparently, and when I went to second-hand shops I did it for free, even though I knew I wasn't looking like someone who was likely to attract anyone.

Travelling to Hastings felt brave. It required a bus ride along the coast and sandwiches in a Tupperware box. There are days when you wake up and you feel stronger, more able, and I had anticipated one would come this week. There were three shops I really wanted to look at. The largest was in the old town and was my main interest. It had rooms. I like a shop with rooms.

* * *

When Jenny left she said it wasn't me, it was her. How many people have said that before? She stayed with me through the first illness. Two years of hospital appointments; chemotherapy, drugs, scans and the sharp irritability that surprised us both when I was given the all clear. We expected happiness to tumble out of relief but in truth I was angry all of the time. I didn't know why. Now I think it was because I knew on some cellular level it was still in me. Hiding. Waiting.

When it came back, and they said it was liver and lungs and they didn't answer the really hard questions, she said she had to go. 'It's my life I am in too,' she said, which sounded like a quote from the sort of film that annoyed me when I wasn't ill and I avoided when I was. And then finally, destructively, 'One day I want to have kids. I am allowed to make that possible.'

* * *

The shop was called Sandy's Antiques Emporium, which was neither descriptive nor resonant, but given the person behind the counter when I walked in looked as though she might be called Sandy, it made some sort of sense. I love the moment when you first walk in; the smell and the colour give you an immediate sense of the place, and the sense I had in Sandy's was of a proper second-hand shop. Things were not bright, there was a faint smell of damp, and the floor was uneven. I don't trust a second-hand shop with an even floor.

The woman behind the counter smiled when the door opened. It was her 'greeting the customer' smile and it reshaped itself when she saw me. I was thin, I wore a brown pull-down hat to hide my hairless head and I suppose my skin was slightly yellow. She recovered herself and said, 'Morning.' I nodded politely but hoped she didn't want to talk. I don't like talking. I like looking.

The shop was divided into lots of different-sized rooms. I don't think it could have been built as a house, it would have made no sense as a place to live. I found myself browsing the first couple of rooms in quite a cursory way as I wanted to see how deep the shop went. The first room had a couple of round tables and a chest of drawers but was dominated by glassware really – glass animals, matching blue vases and a really big snow globe with a model of the Empire State Building in it.

* * *

When Jenny left me, she went on holiday straight away. I thought that made sense. I hoped that she would change her mind when she came back, that she needed some sort of respite from being with me. Of course, if you notice that someone is in need of respite from you then you have a reasonably clear sense of yourself as someone who took far more than they gave to that person. I thought that she would come back. And when she did, I decided I would try very hard to be less difficult to be with, less angry and demanding, less irritable and selfish. Less cancerous. Less me.

After a couple of weeks, I tried to call her. She had changed her number. I did get through to her mother eventually who was polite, if uncomfortable.

'She is moving to New York,' she said. 'A really good job opportunity. She couldn't say no. Not really. It's probably only for two years to start off with…'

Only.

* * *

Sandy's Antiques Emporium was quite deep. It stretched at least five rooms back, carrying on away from the street and any natural light toward darker, fuller, more hidden-away rooms. There I wandered into a small, pink-carpeted parlour that contained an old armchair, some very large painted vases pretending to be Chinese, two wooden trunks that looked heavy and old, an oak desk, small and polished, not big enough to be functional, not pretty enough to be ornamental; a locked glass-fronted bookcase with old books in it and a horrendous grandfather clock that I could not take my eyes off of.

It was easily ten feet tall, too thin to look imposing, but when I touched it it felt very solid, like it was carved from oak. And it was carved in a ridiculous, incongruent African design; ornate, overdone I thought. The carving reached up over the face of the clock like antlers on a deer, or branches on a dead tree. The face itself had no hands or glass, the sides were thick and scratched and the front had a panel carved in a different style, more detailed, more artful, wholly distinct from the rest of the clock.

I looked at the price: £1,245. I tried to imagine the person who would hand over a thousand pounds for that hideous mishmash of wooden, ostentatious clock.

Do I seem grumpy? I am, I know it. Cancer does that – of course it does – but it's the edges of life that make me angry. My cat has started pissing on the kitchen floor. Apparently, the other cats make him anxious. A big ginger cat that was a kitten a couple of months ago and wanted to be my cat's friend seems to have overwhelmed him with his presence and maybe the other cats have joined in. Now my cat, rather than go into the garden to urinate, decides to do it in the kitchen while I am asleep. My cat doesn't care remotely that I am dying.

I was still staring at the giant, ridiculous clock. It took me a moment to turn away, its ugliness was too compelling. I suppose I may have shaken it slightly when I touched it, it is possible I somehow made it move when I let go of the price tag, although I cannot imagine how. I think I remember the first sense I had of movement behind me, or maybe the initial contact it made with the back of my head, and I remember my legs buckling like sticks turning to ash.

I know now it fell on me. I know now it knocked me out. I think it might have been an accident. Or an act of God, in quite a specific sense.

'My name is Gabriel,' said a tall stranger in a black suit. He was wearing loafers with no socks. I instantly disliked him as I instantly disliked most healthy-looking people. To be fair, the dislike tends to pass quickly, although sometimes I find it stays long enough for me to lend it reason. In his case it was because he looked like a singer on a cruise ship who churned out hits from the '80s and thought people wanted to hear them. And he had hair.

I rubbed my head. It didn't hurt. I said, for no good reason, 'My head doesn't hurt.'

'No, but it will.'

'Did the clock fall on me?'

'Yes.'

'Do you work here?'

'It depends on what you mean by here.' He smiled an apologetic smile and shrugged. 'You are currently unconscious, laying under that big clock. To be fair, people are making an appropriate fuss. One is checking your pulse, someone else is calling for an ambulance. You will wake up shortly and wait to see how long it is before attention turns from your physical well-being to the possibility that you might sue. In the meantime, I am here because, well, because you are due some small kindness and I would like to try to help with that.'

He was around my age, I think. As he spoke, he held my gaze. I couldn't tell if he struck me as the type of man who one implicitly trusted, or the type of man who had been on one of those modern communication courses that taught you how to be trusted so you could get away with being a bastard. I don't trust men who go on courses in order to be trusted. He half smiled, almost embarrassed, almost shrugging.

I couldn't think of exactly what to say, and so I said, 'What kind of small kindness?' And then, 'Are you real? Has the cancer reached my brain?'

He smiled. 'No,' he said. 'No, it hasn't.'

But it did occur to me that if that was the cancer talking it could be lying.

'You don't look like I imagine angels look.'

He shrugged.

'Something small, a kindness that helps you feel that you are not wholly unseen, uncared for … And, no, no I am not an angel although, if I may, they are not all they are cracked up to be.'

'Can you make the cancer go away?'

'No.'

'Why not?'

'I don't do miracles; I don't have the power. I don't really have much to offer at all in the grand scheme of things. I'm sort of waiting, there are a lot of us waiting, waiting to see what they will find for us to do, or where they will send me. So I watch people and I saw you and I thought, blimey you are having a bad time, I wonder if could try to help.'

'Can you make Jenny come back to me?'

'No.'

'Why not?'

'Because I can't change other people's lives.'

'What can you do?'

'I could arrange for a small lottery win so that coming on trips like this won't be quite so difficult. I could organise it so that the cats near you stop scaring your cat and he stops pissing on the floor.'

'You know about that?'

'I do, I watched, I felt for you. I think sometimes things are too unfair and they are hidden out of view, aren't they? While I can't do much, I can perhaps help in a small way.'

'Why?'

He shrugged. 'What else is there for someone like me to do, while I wait?'

Someone like him? He looked healthy, self-contained. His hair wasn't coming out, his skin wasn't yellow. His suit looked chosen, he carried it well.

* * *

One of the things I had noticed since the second diagnosis was that I didn't watch people as much as I used to. Jenny and I would separate ourselves from the rest of the world by turning it into television. We'd notice people in the street, watch them on the bus, walk behind them quietly and wait until they were out of earshot and when they were we would turn them into whatever we saw, or colour them with whatever mood we were in. People who got dressed in the dark, people who walked as though their legs didn't quite fit, people who were together but didn't want to be. I don't do that anymore. I found that all I saw when I looked at someone else was their good health and I found that too often it annoyed me. I don't want to die bitter. I don't want to die at all.

* * *

'What can I have?'

Gabriel bit his bottom lip. 'Well, it's not really for me to say…'

'Give me an example.'

'Time,' he said quickly. 'You could have some time back. Time that was yours but you didn't get the most from. Time you spent at bus stops or airports or laying in the dark when you were thirteen and unable to sleep. You have time and you reclaim it.'

'How much?'

'It depends on what you can demonstrate as wholly pointless or wasted, but I reckon if you add it all together probably a month or so.'

'I've wasted more than a month of my life,' I protested.

'Well, bad jobs, awful dates, rubbish films, stuff like that isn't wasted.'

'Says who? And don't say God.'

'Look, I'm not comfortable setting boundaries or concentrating too much on all the things that you can't have. It doesn't feel helpful and, believe it or not, I do understand something of how you feel.'

I looked at him and admit that he did not look like a man who was lying. But then, that is the point of those communication courses that people who work in marketing go on, isn't it?

'Who are you again?'

He sighed, ran his hand through his hair and nodded.

'I'm recently dead myself and I'm in between jobs. They don't really know what to do with me.' He raised his eyebrows upwards suggesting either heaven or the people who lived in the flat above the shop. 'But while they are sorting that out I said I would like to do something and they said what and I said I don't know, something kind…'

'And you are absolutely not an angel?'

'Good Lord no. But I work with them sometimes. I'm smaller than that. Think of me as a volunteer.'

'You're a celestial charity worker?'

He went to say no but stopped. 'Yeah, maybe.'

'Why me?'

I knew why me. Cancer, lonely, poor, afraid, dying, cat that keeps pissing on the kitchen floor. I mean I'm not so removed from reality to imagine that there are not plenty of people on the planet living a harder life or awaiting a harder death, but that perspective doesn't stay in your bones, not the way cancer does. It flits in and out and you try to hold it but you can't. Or I can't. Indeed, it tends to leave me usually around the time the cat pisses on the floor.

I don't have any money. I used to have a job. I worked for a sports agent. I once negotiated a short, albeit fake, marriage for a gay footballer on his last legs who was worried about being accepted in China, a country willing to pay him stupid money because he had once been good. He settled very well, even got a contract extension. I didn't always like my clients but I was quite good at being an agent.

I was particularly good at what we used to call 'negotiating the perks' – adding in the little extras that come at the end of the deal. I got a cricketer a hair transplant once, when he signed to play in the Indian Super League. Everyone thought the deal was done but I knew he was desperate for this treatment, and I made up this story about his hair loss being at the optimal point for transplant during his stay in India and him foregoing hair for a lifetime by signing this contract. The other people were tired and wanted to go home and they just agreed. I was good at that sort of thing; 'getting the honey from the bottom of the jar', my boss used to say. She's not been in touch either.

I can't work now and the sickness benefits are rubbish. I get letters and have to go and be interviewed. Mostly they want to ask when I will be dying. I don't get hungry, which is just as well, really.

Gabriel shrugged. 'You don't seem to me to be having a great time of it.'

'So what can I do with this time?'

'You can have it, now, and you can have it healthy. You can get up from under the clock – I agree you may need some help with that – you can go home, and you will find a card on your kitchen table with a phone number. You call the number and you simply ask for the time promised by

Gabriel and you will have, by my estimate, a very healthy four weeks, two days, five hours, and thirty-two minutes to live out.'

'And I will be healthy?'

'Yes.'

'Is it … is it like a holiday from cancer?'

'Yes, yes it is. Although that does sound like a bad heavy metal song.'

'If you can make the cancer go away…?'

'Why can't I keep it away? I don't have that power, nowhere near. I'm respite, maybe I'm nothing really, maybe they are just humouring me.'

He was trying to be honest. He was probably part of a bigger picture, but I was in the small picture. When you have cancer, you shrink into your own existential postcard. News stories of faraway wars or trade negotiations, they are not for you. Is there anyone who would not love another four weeks? There may be, I suppose, someone who has made their peace, someone who wanted to put the postcard in the bin. I wasn't there yet. In fact, that might have been the problem.

'Any chance of some spending money?'

'Do I look like a fairy godmother?'

'Just a thought.'

I was worried about the money thing. I wondered if I could get a loan – clearly not from the afterlife, but maybe a bank?

'I still think I have wasted more time than four weeks. How do you judge time to be wasted? I went on some awful dates. Hell, I sat through double geography for three years, load of nonsense about cloud formation and tectonic plates.'

'You've said that before, haven't you?'

'Said what?'

'Said "load of nonsense about cloud formation and tectonic plates."'

'No. Maybe. I don't know.'

'You have. It's been part of an anecdote or a joke or something and that is why it doesn't count as wasted.'

'What on earth…?'

'Wasted time is time you never tell stories about. If it has ever formed an anecdote, a piece of conversation, a throwaway line … well then I am afraid it doesn't count as wasted.'

'Who makes this stuff up?' I shouted. I expected the shop owner to hear me and come to the back of the shop and find me under her awful great clock. She didn't.

'Does it matter?' He looked impatient for the first time. It occurred to me that, despite him being here and saying he wanted to help, perhaps he didn't like me.

'It just doesn't seem very long…'

He sighed, looked away, and sucked his lips in. Then he spoke very softly, like he had at the beginning.

'I get that. I understand that you are having a horrible time and that it would be wonderful if someone could offer you a big thing; something like a cure, love, bigger hope. I honestly understand that and I wonder if perhaps offering something small – something that feels almost teasing rather than transcendent – may even make things worse. I honestly wanted to try to make things better, just a little, because I could. Because I have permission, because they are embarrassed about what happened to me and are giving me more than they would…'

'Why are they embarrassed?'

'It doesn't matter. I'm sorry I only have a small gift but for what it is worth I think four weeks of living well, maybe seeing people you care about or things that thrill you … well … I think I would have liked that.'

I thought about Jenny. I thought that maybe I could take out a credit card or two, fly to New York, healthy, and see her. I could show her me and she would fall in love with me again and I would know what that felt like. I would see something other than pity or fear when she looked at me. I would feel her skin on my proper skin, and I would not wonder if she could feel my bones rotting or if she worried about hurting me. And then I thought of her without me, in New York, smiling again.

And I imagined, just for a moment, making love and then I imagined making her pregnant and my smallness didn't scare me, just for a moment as I thought about a child of mine spinning through time, without me. And then I thought of her without me, smiling again.

I looked at the tall embarrassed non-angel. I don't know why, but I had the sense that our time was running out. Maybe because he looked at his wrist even though he was not wearing a watch.

'I may feel ashamed,' I said quietly.

He sighed, sympathetic rather than impatient.

'You seem angry too. I get that, angry makes sense. I'm not suggesting it doesn't. Sorry, does that make me sound like a therapist?'

I ignored the question. If we didn't have very much time it didn't make sense to waste it talking about him. 'I think, I could be wrong, but I think the part that scares me is the abandonment of hope. If I have got to the point where things are so bad that I am negotiating with angels…'

'I'm absolutely not an angel.'

'You know what I mean. If I am negotiating with the afterlife it is because I am on my way there. If respite is all there is, it means that there will be no miracle cure, no last-minute recovery … because that is what you are saying really, isn't it? That the best that God can give me is a holiday from my own demise. Don't get me wrong, I'm grateful – really grateful. In fact, being seen and noticed and thought about, that alone means the world. But it does mean that that is all there is, doesn't it? That I'm dying now?'

He stared at me, impassively. I thought he would nod. He didn't. I didn't take the lack of a visible nod to mean anything.

'And I know I am dying but I suppose I feel as if I am more dead now. Now that the only miracle available is four weeks.'

'Four weeks, five days…'

'Yes.'

I'm not a brave man. I never sought out adventure. When I was well, I was risk-averse and travel tended to feel like a wave of disruption rather than an opening of new doors. The idea of flying to New York to see Jenny didn't fill me with excitement. Seeing her, that did. Holding her, I liked that. But getting there? I wondered if I would be able to claim back the travel time from God, double wasted. And then I wondered if asking Gabriel that question counted as being an anecdote and rendered it lost. I was tired. Being under a giant clock probably didn't help with that but cancer makes you tired, and if you are tired you think differently. If the way you feel is the fuel for what you think then my fuel was discoloured, full of sediment, and stale. It was bound to infect my thoughts.

'Is there anything else I can have? Instead I mean. I'm tired you see.'

He nodded. 'Okay, what sort of thing? I can't do things that specifically require me to move people around, to make them feel things that are not their feelings.'

'Can you do good deeds? Small lottery wins?'

He smiled. 'Yes, I think so.'

'And, dare I ask, can you do small bad deeds? The person who keeps making me come in for interviews about my disability benefits, can you kill her house plants, maybe help her twist an ankle?'

He laughed. 'Probably. It seems like a bit of a waste.'

'Yes, I can see that it does, but it's about power really, isn't it? I have no power and tiny little expressions of justice can be very soothing. Maybe you could give me a handful of those?'

'A bagful of small acts that rebalance some of the injustices you experience?'

'Yes, not many.'

He looked thoughtful. 'How many?'

'Well, it depends how small they are. A twisted ankle, for example. No lasting damage, but the opportunity for the disability assessor to experience a passing disability? That is virtually a gift. How about a couple dozen of those?'

'Are there twenty-four ankles you want to twist?'

This time I smiled. 'There are other little things. The person who got my job when I had to leave, he laughed at my hair coming out at my leaving drinks. Can I give him alopecia? Jenny's best friend ignored me when I called her name outside Costa Coffee two weeks ago. I know she heard me, though she pretended not to. Can I give her ear wax?'

'Do you not feel a little petty?'

I had been a professional negotiator. I had always felt petty.

'Yes, but people are petty in pursuit of relief, aren't they? If you cut in front of someone in your car it's because you are cross about them speeding or buying a BMW or something and you imagine that the crossness will reduce with your tiny act of revenge.'

'But it doesn't.'

'But it might.'

He looked disappointed and unconvinced. 'I don't think I understand what it is you are trying to achieve.'

'I'm trying to make things feel more equal.'

'Ear wax? Twisted ankles?'

I sighed. 'I think I just want to feel a little better about the world before I leave it.'

'And the best way to do that is to make other people feel a tiny bit worse?'

'Quite harmless in the scheme of things,' I said quietly.

He didn't look convinced but he didn't look at his non-existent watch again. And he hadn't completely given up on me. I got the impression that he had hoped for something more straightforward. To offer to do something nice, to receive a grateful smile and to be on his way.

And you have to understand I am not proud of what I did next, but it's that sediment you collect when you feel what I feel and carry what I have to carry. It gathers up and you feel yourself filling with … with what? Bad feelings? Ugliness? The worst bit of you that you had not noticed when you were well? Whatever it was it felt like grey, heavy silt and it filled me now.

I thought about Jenny. I thought of her leaving me, not loving me enough. Of her laughing with new friends in America, not remembering me, not remembering England. Of her walking in Central Park the day they bury me and trying to remember the good times. And then a man asks her if she is okay, and she says she is sad, and I become an anecdote. A sanitised anecdote because who tells someone on what will turn into a first date that they left their last lover because he had cancer? Nobody.

Later maybe, after they have slept together and are drawn toward a little more emotional intensity, then she can talk about how hard it was to stay with someone through cancer, twice, how that changes a relationship, a person. How love becomes replaced by something else. And how she ran out of whatever it was she needed to be the person she thought she was.

And how the guilt eats at you. The terrible guilt. And he would hold her as she cried, not for me, she would not be crying for me, she would be crying for her. And he'd say she did the right thing and they would make love and I would not even be the victim of my own story. I would be someone from whom she was liberated, a stepping-stone on the way to better things. To America, to him, to the babies they might have: Chuck, Belle, fucking Billy Bob.

I want to be a better man. I don't want to think these thoughts, but you can't un-think thoughts. Not when you have this silt clogging up your blood.

'Can I ask a question, please?'

Gabriel nodded.

'If we have sort of agreed in principle to up to twenty-four small acts of God, might I exchange them for one larger one?'

He shook his head slightly. I took it as a sign of disappointment rather than him saying no. I carried on.

'Just in principle, an exchange?' 'I have limited power but, yes, in principle I suppose... Like I said, I want to help.'

I licked my lips and stared at Gabriel. He had gentle eyes. I think he was hopeful for me. That was nice of him, I suppose. I looked away.

'Jenny, my ex, the one in New York?'

'Yes?'

'I want to share one more thing with her.'

He smiled. 'Okay, I can try. What is it?'

'My cancer. Just a little bit of it.'

I heard him sigh and saw him shake his head and mutter something.

Next thing I knew I was not under the clock and someone was handing me a glass of water. They were helping me on to a chair. I kept looking for Gabriel, but he was gone, if he had been there at all.

When I got home there was no card on the table. No phone number to call. The cat had pissed on the floor.

Of course, it was all probably a dream, a delusion brought on by the weight of the clock. But even if that was the case the damage is real, isn't it? Because now I know what I would choose if I had any choices. Now I know who I am. And dying doesn't feel as though it matters quite as much as it did. I wonder if perhaps that was the gift.

The Voice Collector

IN THE BEGINNING God said, 'Let everyone have at least two voices in their head, and let the voices talk out loud so that the owner of that head can hear what they say very clearly. Let the voices not ever be full of wrath, or even a bit sarcastic. In fact,' God said, 'Let the voices be gentle voices, helpful and encouraging. And no jokes. Or not many. Nobody wants a comedian in their head. Not really. Not all the time.'

And everyone did have at least two voices in the beginning. And they were helpful and encouraging, but then things got complicated.

I don't know if the problem was that God stopped watching or perhaps became distracted. Maybe she went and started another world somewhere else, or simply looked the other way, but the voices stopped being kind and they did catch wrath and, worse, some of them became quite spiteful.

Here's my theory. Do you want my theory? I'm going to put it out there while I can because sometimes I can come and go depending on whatever it is that I need to attend to. I can be saying something, concentrating and everything, and then – bang – I'm sort of called away. I have collected a lot of voices and put them in my head and sometimes one or two of them shout and sometimes that distracts me. Anyway, my theory, for what it's worth, is that God has more than one project on the go. We – and by we, I don't mean the voices and me, I mean people, loads of us all over the world – we talk a lot about there being the one God but not so much about her having more than one universe to decorate. We could be just one of the projects she has on the go, couldn't we? Hell, we might have been a prototype or something.

And I'm not complaining or anything. If she has other worlds to put together, do you find yourself wondering how many? Five maybe? Or seventeen? Or fifty-seven? He or she is probably a long way away by now. Assuming space is actually a thing to God. And that would explain why we have never really met aliens if you think about it. If God made us all in a slightly different way, for a different reason, when he or she was in a different mood, he wouldn't want us to meet each other, would he? Or she? I'm not sexist in the way I think of God. Not out loud anyway.

Or what if there are hundreds of worlds, or thousands or hundreds of thousands? That is beyond my imagination, I'm afraid. But what if ours was a restless God, spinning through the universe making worlds out of metaphysical playdough and then moving on? Unafraid of what might happen. Not really bothering to check back in with us to see how things have gone. Maybe she is an improvising God? Maybe she doesn't even keep records? Not that she would need them. Probably.

Anyway, regardless of what God has been up to since the voice thing, let's just concentrate on the voice thing. We all had two voices to begin with: instinctive and logical. We say it when we say we are in two minds, don't we? Scientists talk about the brain having two hemispheres? Sometimes we talk about the heart ruling the head? Philosophers cling to their dualities. Taoists have their Yin and their Yang. All I'm saying is that when everything began, in the beginning if you like, the two things had voices that spoke out loud. To each other. Without fighting. Like good parents.

But then we evolved and the voices learned to be more than they had been because that is what voices do. At first they learned how to win arguments instead of just presenting possible actions, then they started to mock and that meant they stopped working together. Indeed, they became quite oppositional.

I think the voices began to strategise; they were seduced by the prospect of power and then simply by beating the other voice. They learned to trick each other, to paradox arguments, to poke fun at other voices. Some of them learned to shout. Some began to swear. There was grandstanding, posturing, arguing just for the sake of arguing and then the voices went forth and multiplied. They gave rise to more voices, voices that were only angry, only swearing, only violent, and they pretty much did whatever they wanted. And that made for chaos.

The worst ones were the ones who whispered and didn't shut up. The voices – some of the voices, lots of the voices – went past sarcastic into venomous and the heads – some of the heads, lots of the heads – were struggling to hold them in, and that way lies madness. The cruellest voices would not shut up, they were constantly vindictive, gathering just behind the ear. Perpetually unkind.

And that is where I come in. I am, on the face of it, a very ordinary woman. Less than ordinary, some would say. Looking less than ordinary is a gift, by the way. It resides mostly in the coat and, I suppose, the way I wear it. I am not tall and not striking. I am not young or clever or rich. I am not pretty. I never wear make-up. I face away from people when I walk, my gaze slightly downward. I have what might be considered a slight hunch, which makes sense, given what I am carrying. My hair is a simple mousey brown, un-dyed but clean. If you want to go unseen have clean and un-sculpted hair.

But if you have a voice in your head that is harmful, violent, ugly, aggressive, I can take it from you. Put it in a box inside the warehouse in my head, which is both full of other peoples' ugly assaulting voices, and limitless in its capacity to store the nasty bastards. I don't charge. I do it for love. Or kindness. Or because I can and it does some good. I know, how un-modern am I! Sue me.

I'm not an angel. I mean, I don't have a contract or anything, but I am more than a good woman, or a woman who does good deeds. It's not for me to call myself a superhero or anything, and I don't expect a comic strip, although a guest appearance in someone else's might be nice. Dinner with Spiderman maybe. Or the blind one? What's his name? Anyway, it is a power this thing I do, collecting and imprisoning the cruel invasive voices, and it helps.

I have hundreds of them. Thousands. More probably. I can't count them. If I was going to count them I'd have to let some of them out of the boxes, and that would be dangerous.

My head, this less than ordinary head, is full of voices. Not so much a prison as a wildlife park. The people you call psychotic who get better? Sometimes that's me. The people you call schizophrenic? I haven't got to that yet. I'm flypaper for voices. Clearing up God's mess. I'm going to tell you about one. He, for he is a he, is a right bastard. You don't have to thank me.

So I'm on this psychiatric ward and I am pushing the trolley that someone once called the mobile library, but which is now a small table with casters that has twenty-five books and some very old magazines on it, and it is my job to hand out reading material to patients. I get paid to travel around different hospitals with a vanload of books that are largely donated; lots of fiction obviously, some biography, not much poetry. I go onto wards and ask people what they fancy. Even if they don't want any books they like to come and chat because it breaks the monotony. Anyway, this ward smells of cabbage and disinfectant. It's clean but it looks a mess. The furniture is modern but the chairs are low and thus not terribly functional or comfortable. In short, it was designed by a committee and there was a short person on the committee. I knew my way around these places, and I knew that I would become familiar over a few weeks as the book lady. I also had the sense that they would recognise me as one of their own, even if they didn't think it out loud.

Vanessa was her name. She wanted to be demure but couldn't quite pull it off. She was thin, pale, awful skin. Every time I saw her she had what looked like the same three boils on her young face that simply seemed to move around. She looked like someone who ate by default. She had greasy black hair that often hung in straggly, shoulder-length ringlets and made her look like a caricature of an orphan. But sometimes she tied it up and, despite the spots, she looked pretty. Bright-eyed, even. Although I got the sense the eyes were bright because they were damp from crying when she was alone and scared.

She didn't socialise with the other patients very often, but when she did she attracted a nice attention. The young mad boys with their drug-induced psychoses and medically-dulled senses wanted her to like them but weren't ugly about it. Together they were a gentle, fragile little band of waifs. Aware enough to know that each had their struggles, too locked into their own heads to do anything overly kind with that awareness.

I had the sense that the two boys she was friendly with would both find their way. Yes, they heard voices. Yes, when I stood close to them I heard them too, but they were background voices, like the annoying chatter you hear at a party that isn't going well. And they were fading, I could tell. The boys had the option to make friends with their voices. Or they could learn to quieten them. Or they could just stop smoking rubbish drugs. Vanessa didn't have that range of choices. Vanessa made me sad.

She named her voice Stan. I can't tell you the things he said, not all of them, I don't want to put that voice in the world. And I can't tell you to imagine the vilest of things because you can't imagine vile like this.

The first time she cut herself, when she was fourteen, it was because Stan told her to. When she cut a slice of flesh the size of a two-pence coin out of the side of her neck it was because Stan told her to and because that exact place was where a man had put his mouth when she was eight. He had smelt of beer and bonfires.

Stan told her to cut her legs – that if she cut deep enough then one day it would let the shame out, but in the meantime it would remind her that she deserved whatever she got. Because she is dirty, a disappointment to everyone who knows her, and when people see her, before she has even spoken, they know she is dirty, worthless. Dried blood on rotten flesh. They know because Stan said they know, he didn't have to tell them. They can see it.

I saw her try to pull her own hair out once, perhaps imagining that Stan was attached to the roots and would emerge with the thick handful of hair. She made her scalp bleed. I think I heard Stan laughing. If I heard it, she did.

The next time I went in with the books I found Vanessa sitting in a corner mumbling to herself, talking to Stan. It crossed my mind that maybe they were trying to make friends. She wasn't shouting or pleading. When I got closer,

I realised she was trying to explain herself. That it wasn't her fault, that she knew she was dirty and she should have hidden, but she was eight and no, that was no excuse but there was nowhere to hide and, again, she was sorry. It was important to try to help but also not to scare her. I was just the book lady, after all. But there was always one way that helped with that. I had done it before with other people, and they were relieved when I did. So, one day, when she was on her own, I went up to Vanessa and said gently, 'I can hear him too.'

Stan couldn't help himself. 'No, she can't. She wants to fuck you too.' I shook my head and said, 'Yes, I can, and no, I promise I really don't.'

She stared at me. Stan was quiet for a moment and I said, 'That is an evil voice, Vanessa. A spiteful, lying voice. You don't deserve that in your head. Let me take him from you. I have a place he can go.' She carried on staring, began to shake her head.

I heard Stan say, 'Fuck off, knob head.'

I smiled and said, 'He's scared of me, Vanessa. He's just a bully. Another bully. Enough now.' I reached out my hand. I didn't touch her head, but I felt the faintest trace of a stray hair on my fingers as I lifted Stan from her skull. He said the C word and I held him in my hand for a moment so he knew I could and then I put him in a box just behind my left ear, in a pile of boxes, near the bottom, which took some rearranging because there were a lot of boxes.

I'm not immune. At night I can hear them sometimes but I can't make out what they are saying, and I don't care. I know what they are and where they belong.

Sometimes I have bad thoughts. I imagine bumping into a man with bad teeth who smells of beer and bonfires. I'd ask Stan if he recognised the man and I would know if he lied, and then I would ask Stan if he would like to come out of his box, if he would like to have the man to talk to, to play with, to fuck up. I've never done that. It's not my place, I don't think.

Mostly I worry about what will happen when I die. Will the voices die too? Or will they float off into the ether looking for heads to refurnish? That is when I wish God was not so far away. But wishing doesn't make any kind of difference.

Vanessa cried. When I took the voice away, she cried. I happen to know that getting out of the hospital was a challenge. Those places are not built for recovery. They don't believe in cures, so when they come along some of the people who work there imagine they are simply dealing with new symptoms. But Vanessa was in no rush. She was discharged, and they helped her find somewhere to live, and a job in a pet shop. I saw her again, from a distance, sitting outside a coffee shop. She was with other people and she was smiling. She didn't see me. And she only heard the people who were speaking to her. And perhaps the music that was playing in the shop, but nobody really listens to that, do they?

Resurrection Boy

I MUST HAVE been ten, coming up to eleven, when I found out. I was at school, sitting at the edge of the playground – the concrete patch of grey that tended to be occupied by dinner ladies, the nervous younger children and girls with skipping ropes. The rest of us swarmed over the surrounding playing field. I was waiting for my friends to come with the football. They had school dinners, I had sandwiches because my Dad wouldn't let us accept free school dinners, which was annoying because, as Mum said, you'd never see him turn down a free drink, but he said that was different, that was decency, not charity and he said it like it was a law. I used to have white bread sandwiches filled with those horrible soft cheese triangles and a chocolate biscuit. I was hungry as soon as it was gone.

Anyway, I was sitting on the grass scratching away at a patch of dry dirt with a broken stone. Now, when I try to picture it, I think the dirt was so scorched it probably felt nearly dead, like the ground had no hope of growing anything again even if the rest of the field was forever covered in grass. I was digging a cross-shaped hole quite purposefully, but I would have been thinking nothing at all. I was just waiting for my friends and doing something with my hands as I did so.

Sitting near me were three younger boys playing with a magnifying glass. One of them was holding the glass so that it caught the sun and burnt whatever it was they were gathered around. I didn't give it very much thought. I assumed they were setting fire to grass or a spider or something. but it was what boys do. I remember that the boy with the magnifying glass was wearing NHS spectacles, and appeared studious rather than bad. Like he was conducting an experiment. The other boys were shouting; one of them in particular was getting very excited. 'That's cruel,' I said. Not because I felt anything or cared but because I was bored and ten and they were loud and eight.

'It's just cruel,' I said again, trying to sound mature. For better or for worse I had broken the moment. 'So? It's dead anyway!' shouted the excited boy triumphantly, and he ran off, perhaps to find something else to hurt.

The boy with the glasses looked sheepish and uncertain. His friend, the one who had sat beside him quietly watching like another scientist, or a psychopath, blushed. The one with glasses tapped him on the side and said, 'Come on.' And they got up and wandered off. They didn't look back. When they caught up with the loud one, they all started running.

I got up and went over to where they had been sitting. There were four or five blades of burnt grass and a dead spider. It was small and had had a leg burnt off before it had been killed. I picked the burnt grass, tossed it away and rolled the spider over. It was charred and curled up. I must have been tired of waiting, or curious about the texture of dead spiders, or I may have wondered about heat retention in dead spiders, although I doubt it.

Then I picked it up. It felt dead like a stone and light like a feather. It felt of nothing in my hand. I remember staring at it. I remember the sun was shining, and my heart was beating, and I was breathing. And the spider moved.

I felt it like a hair on my hand. I put it down on the ground as gently as I could and the spider walked away. As it walked, I think it was concentrating on getting used to having one less leg and not being dead. Then it moved more quickly. It didn't occur to me that spiders could withstand the heat of the sun. That they were indestructible like cockroaches or my Uncle Vince who fell off of a cliff and survived and then got hit by a car three weeks later and survived, and then got stabbed with scissors by Auntie Val and survived. It hadn't been in a spider coma, it had been dead. And now it was alive.

Instinctively, and this feels significant now in a way it didn't before, I decided not to tell anyone that I could bring dead spiders back to life. I don't think I decided this as the result of very much thinking. Rather I suspect I didn't tell my friends because I had waited a long time to play football and I was not going to do anything that meant having to wait longer. But mainly I think I was afraid that the tiny possibility of personal magic would disappear as quickly as it had come if I had to demonstrate it to other ten-year-olds, particularly if it didn't work. I stored away my secret power next to my intention to be an astronaut and captain of the England football team.

This feels like it was a long time ago now. It isn't really, but it feels like it, and in truth I can't remember if I thought very much when I was ten, let alone what the thoughts were. What does feel clear to me is that I carried my secret very lightly in those days. Or, I should say, I don't remember thinking very much about it at all for a couple of years. Although I didn't get around to dismissing or doubting it either. I think the fact that I could restore life to dead spiders seeped into my skin and became a truth – a truth I didn't feel the need to visit, reflect on or test.

The next time it visited me was when I had a cousin come to stay. He was like a hurricane in brown acrylic, charging around the place, bumping into things and bouncing off them when they broke. He was a little bit younger than me and he seemed to resent that, so he jumped on me and started fighting, which may have been his way of saying 'Hello, let's play', but I was reading a comic, so I hit him. I don't think he had ever been hit before and it shocked him. He threatened me from behind his mum and he cried and kicked the sofa, which was a mistake because my mum was there and she didn't tolerate furniture abuse, so he ran into our small garden where he brooded and, unbeknown to me, killed whatever bugs he saw by stamping on them.

Later, after he had gone, I was in the garden and noticed three squashed earwigs. I remembered my spider resurrection and I may have thought about walking away in order to keep my sense of self as special and untested. But I didn't, because I didn't want my cousin to have had the power to kill earwigs. I bent down and touched the least squashed. I moved it around half-heartedly, uncertain. It was brown with a lighter coloured head that made it look transparent. It was more than dead, it was destroyed. And then it moved. It kicked its legs, so I rolled it over and it stood. For a moment I wondered if the movement had simply been the breeze, but the earwig walked. And then I mended its friends.

I don't remember exactly how I felt after that. I suspect I may have been more aware of the ridiculousness of what I had done than I had been before. I may even have been afraid, and I probably wanted to tell my mum because I tended to tell her everything. But it was the point in my life where I needed a secret and on some level this seemed perfect. Keeping it did no harm to anyone and sharing it had no real benefit.

The difference, after that second time, was the fact that I no longer hid from my secret. I didn't store it behind my liver where nobody could see it. Instead, I tested it. I tested it on spiders, daddy long-legs, woodlice, one big black beetle, and some houseflies. I brought them all back to life. On one occasion I caught a spider and dropped it into a cup of water. I watched it struggle until it died, and I left it in the cup for an hour. I came back to it, took it in my hand, gently touched it with the tip of my finger. I saw a glow like a cheap sparkler through a misted window, and the spider was alive again. Damp, confused, if a spider is capable of confusion, but alive.

It was around this time that my father was diagnosed with cancer. I think that is one of the reasons why my memory of the time before the diagnosis is poor. Cancer draws your attention. The time before cancer was a blur and I was a child. After cancer everything had an electricity running through it, which made it more vivid.

It was cancer of the bladder, but when they said that you knew from the end of the word 'cancer' that there would be no full stop after the word bladder.

We were in our living room when he told me. A tiny room with a chair and matching sofa. The sort of thing that used to be part of a three-piece suite but there was no room for the third part. The sofa and chair always faced the TV and the electric fire, so facing each other was hard. We were used to sitting beside each other in our family.

Mum was standing beside him, looking resolute and baggy-eyed. She had a way of standing taller in the face of difficulty, and she faced difficulty a lot. Dad, who was sitting where he always sat in the brown-flecked armchair, spoke quietly and with a kink in his shoulders. As he lent toward me, he already looked defeated. Mum pulled back her shoulders as though she was preparing them for the weight of her husband and son. I didn't cry. I looked at them both and thought crying was not going to help. Instead I mumbled: 'It will be okay.' And I resolved to stop playing at rescuing insects and learn how to save my Dad.

I started with a mouse. In my head it was a big jump from a spider to a mouse, but I think I needed to see as quickly as possible if my power only applied to insects. We were at my Nan's house. She was my Dad's mum and she took the cancer very badly. She said it should have been her, and although it was a dramatic and empty thing to say I think she meant it. 'Nobody should outlive their children,' she said.

My Mum didn't say much when we were round there. On the way home though, she did say, 'It's not like anyone bloody chose it, is it? We didn't fill in a bloody application form and put your Dad's name on it instead of your Nan's.'

Anyway, Nan had a cat and the cat brought in a mouse. The mouse was either dead or doing a very good impression of dead. It was lying limp beside the cat with blood on the back of its neck. Nan stood up, moved away and opted to offer up a commentary on the meaning of the cat bringing the mouse in. 'It's the people next door. They keep rabbits and rabbits attract mice.' This made no sense to me at all. 'It's okay,' I said. 'I've got it.'

I picked up the mouse and carried it through the kitchen and out into Nan's garden. I didn't want them to watch me, so I said loudly, 'Make sure the cat stays in there.' I took it to the end of the garden, stroked its head, and let my finger linger at the point where its neck folded. Not because that is where I decided you needed to re-inject life, but because there was a divot there that fitted my finger. The mouse twitched. I put it down and it ran off. When I went back in my Mum made me wash my hands and my Nan ruffled my hair like I was seven.

Remember my cousin? He had a rabbit. I killed it with the footrest of a pogo stick and then I revived it with my thumb. It took me ages to get the blood off the pogo stick.

I decided to move on to a kitten but couldn't actually bring myself to kill one, so instead I killed a really old arthritic cat who sometimes limped slowly across our garden. I tempted it into the house with a tin of tuna when Mum and Dad were at the hospital. I suspect that the fact they had both seemed nervous before leaving the house served as an incentive to me. When I suffocated the cat under a large cushion, I put my whole body weight on it. I could hear a crack when it stopped struggling, and I was crying but I thought of my Dad and I kept repeating under my breath, 'It will be okay, Dad. It will be okay, Dad.'

When I brought the cat back to life I swear he didn't limp as much as he had before, although he never walked through our garden again. If he ever saw me he ran and hid like a young cat that didn't have arthritis, but had had fear imprinted upon its furry soul.

I had planned to get a summer job as a volunteer at the local vets but Dad's cancer was getting worse; it had spread to his bones and to his liver and I was worried that I was running out of time. So I wrote to the zoo. What I wanted to say was, 'Dear Zoo, do you have any really ill monkeys or even a gorilla I could kill and then resurrect, please?'

Instead I wrote, 'I have a deep and long-held desire to be a zookeeper and wonder if you have any voluntary work I could do over the Christmas period?'

Mum and Dad were confused that I would offer to do voluntary work over the holidays. I think Dad was hurt. He never said it, but I could tell he was thinking it would be our last Christmas together, and surely I would want to be with him as much as I could. I did, and I said I did, but you don't take away hurt with words. Not real hurt. I think Mum thought I was avoiding things. Hiding from the cancer, like that could work. I didn't have any time for that view of the world, I still don't. I think I grew up a lot that Christmas. Zoos tend to be full of volunteers, but not at Christmas. I asked about sick animals on my second day and I was told about Roland, the old silver-backed gorilla who had cancer and who would have been perfect, but he had died a couple of days before I started and been cremated. Yes, the zoo had cremation facilities. No, I didn't want to see them although I thanked them for the offer. Meanwhile, back at home the nurse was coming in most days. Dad was getting thinner and he held himself still when he sat in his chair as though he were balancing a cup of hot water on the top of his head and was afraid of spilling it. When I wasn't at the zoo, I sat beside him on the pouf watching TV repeats of old comedies that didn't make us laugh. He asked me about the zoo, and at first I didn't like talking about it because I was embarrassed about being there rather than with him, but I began to tell him about my days and how I liked being busy and he smiled. I think he understood that. I didn't tell him about the sick monkey though. It didn't seem appropriate.

I didn't like the monkeys. I think I didn't like them because they had arms. I know that sounds ridiculous but it's the truth. And I didn't like the way they looked at me, as if they could see something about me that spiders or mice couldn't. And when they screamed, particularly the sick one whose name was Tony, it was like being hit in the face with a breakfast tray. I don't think Tony trusted me but I could live with not being trusted by a sick monkey, and if it worried me that he might sense something in me that alarmed him, I told myself that he would be grateful for it when the time came.

Tony didn't die quickly, and my Dad was not getting any better. In fact, he was beginning to disappear into his chair and blend with the worn tan fabric. His arms became so thin, like squashed coat hangers wrapped in tissue paper. I began to think he might die before the monkey and I would have to go to him unready. What if I needed to be ready? What if I needed to believe and for that needed more evidence? What if I needed the practice? Helping Tony toward the end was not an option. For one thing the damn monkey hated me, and even as it lay on its straw bed too weak to eat and too tired to move anything other than its head, it stared at me like I was a trick waiting to happen. For another, the vet never left me alone with Tony. In fact, the vet never left me alone with any of the sick animals.

Anyway, eventually one Thursday evening, the week before Christmas, Tony died. His eyes were wet and old, and he had collected a white mucus at the side of his unmoving mouth. When the vet looked at his mouth his teeth were yellow and black, and Tony's fur was dull and matted. He died an organ at a time.

The vet sighed and murmured something about paperwork. She asked if I wanted to see the cremation. I shrugged. I think she thought I was uncomfortable around death. In truth I didn't anticipate there would need to be one. While she did her paperwork, I busied myself by clearing up. I was sweeping when she left to tell the chief warden, and I put down the broom and sat beside the dead monkey's body. I touched his head with my left hand and his cold, bristly chest with my right. It seemed to take longer than the cat or the mouse. Certainly longer than the rabbit who sprang back to life very quickly, but it may have just seemed longer because I was worried about the vet coming back, or one of the keepers coming in. As it turned out that was not what I needed to worry about.

When the vet came back, I had my hands on the monkey and may have looked as though I was praying. I hadn't noticed her coming in, but I heard a cough and ignored it. I was concentrating, staring at Tony's chest, waiting for it to move. When Tony came back to life, he screamed like nothing I had ever heard – not an exhalation of death but a primal screech of fury. The vet said something, it may have been 'oh my God'. I wasn't paying attention because the monkey sat up. Not like a monkey but like an actress from one of those 1940s horror films. Tony looked at me. He was angry. He stood up, jumped up and down and hit me on the head. The vet muttered something else. It may have been 'fuck'. From her point of view the monkey was mocking her. From my point of view, he was hitting me hard on the head with his annoying arms and screeching like an asthmatic fire engine.

I heard the keeper run in and the vet shouted 'tranquilise' and the keeper shouted, 'I thought you said he was dead, for Christ's sake!'

I saw the dart in Tony's side and I expected him to collapse, but he got three more slaps off first and then I watched him fall to the floor. If I had the power to take away life in the same way as I can take away death I would have used it on that bloody monkey. My arms hurt, my head hurt, my shoulder really hurt. Angry undead monkeys hurt, but I had done what I set out to do. It is fair to say that perhaps I had not taken the monkey's feelings as seriously as I might have, but compared to what that meant for my Dad I really didn't care.

Mum said I wasn't allowed to work at the zoo for a while, which suited me. She said I needed to recover and who knew monkeys were so nasty, but in truth Dad was very ill now and she saw risk everywhere. We were vulnerable. Cancer proved it. The monkey just confirmed it.

I wasn't ready when he died. I thought I had more to do, that I needed more practice, that I still had some time. But he went into hospital on the Thursday and he died at four o'clock Friday morning, the day before Christmas Eve.

Mum had been with him until nine o'clock Thursday night, and when he was asleep she came home to me. They phoned her at 4:30 am and asked if she wanted to come in. She said no. Instinctively she thought, 'Why would I wake my fifteen-year-old son and take him to see his father's dead body? How can that help?' She didn't know that I really, really wanted to see him. That I could bring him back to life.

She told me at 6:00 am. She phoned Nan first. They both had crying of their own to do. I think now that she put off telling me because for some part of her he wasn't quite dead until he stopped being my Dad. I remember her sitting on my bed and I knew when I saw her that he was dead. I said, 'I need to see him.'

She said, 'We will,' but I didn't want to wait. I hadn't waited since the drowned spider, which was ages ago. What if my power only worked when the life that had left was still quite near? What if they needed to be warm? What if it was going to be too late? I didn't cry, I did beg.

'Please, Mum, I need to see him. I need to help him.'

And that made her cry. It was a stupid thing to say. It made me sound ridiculous, mad, a child. She said, 'Oh baby,' and put her arms round me. I let her hug me and then I whispered, 'Please, Mum. Please let's go and see him.'

She drew back. She had a wet face and baggy eyes. 'Okay,' she said. 'I'll phone them and tell them we are coming.'

We got a taxi. I'd never been in a taxi before and when it pulled up outside the house the next door neighbours looked out of the window. They knew what it meant. Everyone knew what a taxi down our street meant. The car smelt of hoovering and chewing gum and I didn't talk. It was grey outside, so I stared out of the window and ground my teeth. I wondered what Mum would say, what the hospital would say, when I brought him back. I wondered what not having my secret would mean, what being known as the boy who resurrects dead things, dead people might be like. But I didn't think about those things properly – not with any imagination anyway. I just thought about the relationship between me and dead things and about making my Dad breathe again, making him live.

Here is what I remember. Stepping on to the ward, the lights were bright, the floor was shining and so were the walls. I remember noticing I had a beating, throbbing chest for the first time since cross country when I was twelve. I remember passing two nurses who paid us no attention and I remember glancing at my Mum and noticing she had her shoulders pinned back, clutching her handbag close. I could see her knuckles were white and her eyes were more open than eyes should be.

The Ward Sister walked down the ward and met us. She was a small dark-haired lady with big brown eyes and a face liked a kind stoat. She was older than she looked, I think; I could see grey flecks in her hair and she looked as though she was trying to disguise the sort of tiredness that comes with having to do hard things for a very long period of time. She said softly, 'I am so sorry for your loss,' which could have sounded almost perfunctory if she hadn't followed it with, 'He hasn't been with us very long but we had a sense of him as being a kind man. Polite and, dare I say, brave.'

'Thank you,' Mum said quietly.

'Can I see him please?' I hadn't planned to speak but the words came anyway.

The Sister looked at me for a few moments. 'Of course.' she said quietly and she turned and led us across the ward to a side-room.

I wondered if my words had sounded hurried or griefless or perhaps even boyish, but I was concentrating on what I knew I was about to do, and I knew that everything was about to change. And anyway, all thoughts left me when I stepped into the small side-room and saw my Dad's body laying still on the bed. The blinds were half-closed so the room was not bright and the only thing I could smell was sweetened soap.

The most striking thing was how clean and ordered everything was. The nurses had done whatever it is they do, and I fleetingly wondered if whatever it involved might make him less available to me, but again I let the thought pass. Mum stood still. She had walked into the room and stopped about four feet from the bed. It occurred to me for the first time that she did not want to see her dead husband. She was here for me, because I told her I needed to be here.

I walked over to my Dad and sat on the plastic chair beside the bed. His hair was combed, his eyes were closed. His pyjamas, new and bought for hospital, were clean and done up. I put my hand on his arm and I heard my mother say: 'Don't touch him,' and then immediately, 'Sorry, love.' I ignored her and moved my hand to his chest. I could feel the cold permeating through the pyjamas. I stood up and lifted my other hand to his head and I waited.

I don't know how long passed. It may have been five minutes, it may have been less, but Mum broke the silence from the middle of the room. 'Come on, son. Say goodbye.'

I ignored her, I think I pressed my hand down more, I may have whispered, 'Dad'.

'The nurses need to get on with their work, son.' This summed up my Mum, she didn't want to be any bother and she didn't want people to think she made things difficult.

'Just a minute,' I said. I heard the Sister who was standing near my mum say quietly, 'It's okay, there is no rush.'

Eventually I felt my mum put her hand on my shoulder and whisper, 'Come on, son, please. It's okay, he knows.'

To this day I don't know how long I was there before she gently pulled me away, and I don't know what it was he knew or what it was she meant. I did know, because I would never have left that room if I hadn't, that my power had failed me the only time it mattered. I did not save my Dad. I saved an angry monkey, an old cat, some spiders, and a rabbit. I saved lives that I bumped into or crossed paths with. I wondered later if I had the power to save lives of things that I did not love – if caring was my kryptonite – but it wasn't until I was seventeen or eighteen that I thought about finding out.

I did not try to save anything after Dad died. I was numb for a very long time. I went through the motions a little. I left school, went to college, I was doing a Diploma in Electrical Installation. I can't say I loved it, but I liked its logic. I liked being able to see with my eyes the connections I made with my hands. Anyway, I was walking home from college one day and I found a dead fox in the gutter. There is a space in the middle of our village which gives the impression of a pause – a stretch of road of maybe fifty yards with no buildings on either side of the road apart from a garage and what used to be a barn. We lived in one part of the village, the bus stop to the college was on the other side, and the fox was lying right in the middle of this quiet empty space.

It was not long dead. The blood on its head was not congealed and its eyes were open and wet. I looked around to see if the road was busy; there were very few cars and the only other people I could see were two schoolgirls on the other side of the road a little way behind me. They were too far away to see what I was doing and too young to care and so I crouched down, more out of curiosity than anything else, and I tentatively touched the fox on the back of its neck. I felt something soften and I let the softness warm my fingers. The fox lifted its head and I stepped back. It got to its feet and walked into the road. There was a car coming and it braked sharply. The fox jogged across the road and off into the field opposite where it disappeared behind a hedge. I stared at my hand, and when I looked up the girls, and the car driver were staring at me.

I do realise that at some point in all of this I should have thought about how I might ultimately use my ability to do good. How I could save people or animals even though I had failed to save my Dad. But the truth is I didn't. After Dad died, I don't think I had much sympathy for the world and so it got smaller. In fact, I don't think I had any sense of a relationship between me and the universe. I didn't really think any further than the relationship between me and my life-giving fingers. I think – and over time this idea became set very firmly inside me – that failing and loving went together. I instinctively came to feel that the lives that had mattered the least had returned the quickest. And so, I wondered, what if the limits of my power were not established according to species but rather according to depth of feeling? That made some sort of sense. I had after all resurrected a monkey that was old, with heart failure, liver failure and riddled with cancer, when I really didn't like the monkey any more than it liked me.

It did occur to me that it might have been good to talk about these things, but the obvious person would have been Mum, and she seemed more brittle than she had been. She had lost weight after Dad died and I think holding her shoulders back all the time was taking it's toll. And anyway, at the back of my mind I couldn't bear the thought of me telling her, showing her what I could do and her looking at me wondering why I had not managed to bring back Dad.

There was a part of me that wanted to be able to forget it all. To get on with life, to qualify, get a job, maybe meet someone, certainly look after Mum, too; be more than someone who gives life back to spiders. But forgetting is absurd. I was riddled with the thing the way Dad had been riddled with cancer. It filled me and I had come to completely believe in it, to the point of being devout.

I was walking home from college one evening, three or four weeks after resurrecting the fox. It was coming up to two years after Dad had died and I was thinking about Christmas. It was cold and we had the tree up even though it was a bit half-hearted. I didn't like Christmas because it was full of the spaces my Dad should be in, but Mum and I had this sort of unspoken hellish agreement where we pretended we were having fun and gave each other permission to not have to pretend too dramatically.

I saw two boys in front of me. They were about fourteen or fifteen and were in school uniform. They kept turning around and looking at me. At first I didn't care but it became so obvious and so recurrent that it began to irritate me. I began to recognise them, or at least one of them, as the boy with the NHS-style glasses from the playground when I was little, one of the kids who had been killing the spider with the magnifying glass. I walked with my hands in my pockets and paid them no attention, even though they continued to glance back. My sense was that they might not recognise me from primary school, but the village is quite small and they may know me as the boy whose Dad died. They split up at the end of the main road, and I found myself following the boy with the spectacles. I don't remember picking up the brick. I don't remember if it was windy, I didn't see the branches of the trees. I tend to look down when I walk. Partly I like to avoid people, and not looking at them helps with that, but mostly I don't want to tread on any ants. Sometimes I look up. I could see the stars because the sky was cloudless. There were no birds. When this started, when I gave myself permission to think about my power, I used to look for birds and wonder why nobody ever saw them fall dead from the sky. You'd think, given the number of birds there are in the world some of them would die while they were flying and would just drop to the earth and land on unlucky people. I used to imagine a dead bird landing beside me, and I would lay my hands on it and it would jump up, be confused, fly off and try to catch up with the other surprised-to-see-him birds. It never happened. It would have been good if it had though, especially if someone had seen, someone good. Someone who was impressed and not afraid.

I remember feeling something like indignation. I have this gift – I don't claim to have earned it, I certainly didn't design it – but I have it and perhaps someone somewhere gave it to me for a reason. If I haven't worked out what that is for yet, is that my fault? Or if I have failed to use it properly, fully, is that my fault? Who loses because of that?

Only me, me and my Dad. And my Mum. And maybe other Dads and Mums who I fail to help, because I don't know how to.

This thing, it resides inside me and it is remarkable. It transcends all the usual nonsense we resort to in order to distinguish ourselves from each other; our charm or our skills or our shoes. How many friends we have, how well known we become. I have the ability to bring the dead back to life. People have started religions over less. I have felt this power and I haven't shown anybody. I remember thinking that that is a crime by omission, which my Mum says is just another way to lie.

So I need to not lie.

I started to walk faster and I had stopped looking at the sky. The boy was just in front of me now. I could hear him breathing but he didn't turn around. I imagined the disdain he had for me – the quiet boy with the dead father who worried about spiders, the boy with no friends. He was smaller than I expected. I think maybe everyone is. He had gloves on. It was cold after all. And I suppose I realised that I had known for a little while where this would lead. I wasn't happy about it, but then this wasn't just about me.

I felt the brick in my hand, and I fixed my stare on the top of his thin brittle skull. I remember thinking that I should try to avoid breaking his glasses if I could. It would be noiseless and quick and afterwards, yes, afterwards he will be right as rain. Confused no doubt, afraid maybe, but perfectly alive and with quite a tale to tell. And I will have my first believer.

Immaculate Conception

MY LATE MOTHER told me of my immaculate conception when I was fourteen.

The obvious and, dare I say, lazy observation made by one girlfriend in my formative years was that this explained my Messiah complex, but really that was more of a niggling aside than biological assessment or piercing insight.

On the rare occasion I repeated the story to someone I was close to, the thing that made me blush wasn't the clunking religiosity or the belief bordering on delusion that underpins it, but rather what it revealed about my mother's occasional lack of boundaries. I may not be the best judge of what is 'normal' in the world, but I'm not sure every child was told about the sexual mechanics that led to their conception. Sometimes the loneliness overwhelmed her, I think, and her secrets would slip from her pores. And it was my job to catch them, as gently as I could, for fear they, like her, would pass through the world otherwise unseen.

I'm not going into detail. This part of this story isn't mine, not really. However, she maintained that she and my father did not have sex in the encounter that led to my conception. Not proper sex.

'There was fumbling,' she said, 'and people may have been touched,' which conjured up a crowd scene no fourteen-year-old wants in their head, but she swore there was absolutely and completely no sex.

It was the early 1960s, although there was none of your swinging, liberated, 'three people having a party and everyone looking for it' nonsense. It was still post-war Britain where

I grew up, in everything except ration books and the numbers on the calendar, and in that sort of community – working class and authoritarian – sex was very much for married people. As, of course, was pregnancy. Being pregnant, unmarried, alone, and poor while retaining a sense of innocence that made you seem dishonest and foolish burnt a shame into my mother that never really left her. And so denial made some sort of sense to me. More so than an immaculate conception, anyway.

Not that her version of the world helped her very much. She never had the confidence to spread the word about the sexless conception; she chose to gather shame instead.

My mother was capable of absorbing shame the way sponges absorb water, and she became swollen as a result. She embraced her failings with an enthusiasm that verged on ascetic. She poured her emotions into her perceived faults, which inflated them and made them more visible. She shared her uncertainty and her loneliness and self-consciousness that, I noticed as I grew older, made other people irritable with her. Too much emotion can drive people away. In later years I couldn't tell if she believed she deserved loneliness or if she felt other people had let her down so often that she simply didn't want them too close. Her life became a recurrent flinch from the expected hurt induced by others. Except me, of course, which one or two therapists might have considered the whole point.

But when I was a child I only knew how much my mother embraced motherhood. She said, and I believed her, that the only thing she ever wanted to be was a mum. So, when she fumbled with my subsequently absent and irrelevant father-to-be, I thought beyond the delusion of immaculate conception. Instead, I saw a woman whose very being craved a baby to grow and who knew her time was running out. She was thirty-eight when she had me. My father left for the last time before I had turned two, and he had been barely present before that.

Her other, more respectable story was how close her baby came to death. With a vagueness she would revel in fifty years later, she would say she did not know what nearly killed her new born son. 'They said you had a faulty heart.' And later, 'It was something to do with your kidneys, I think. Or it may have been your liver.' All she knew was that they had called the hospital chaplain in order that I could be named before I died so that God would know what to call me, that the doctor had said there was no more to be done, and that the nurse had told her to pray. Her baby was nearly lost and she could barely breathe. I often wondered why she was not comforted by the idea that God would not waste an immaculate conception by taking the baby he gave her back on the first day, unless of course it was a mistake. I did ask her but she looked at me as if I were a fool. I was. My mother's God does not make mistakes.

Anyway, I survived.

Forever burdened by the miracles of conception and survival, I never produced anything in the world to justify the generosity of the universe. I didn't discover a cure for cancer or stop any wars or write *Young Americans* or *King Lear*, and I am yet to slow global warming, although I do have a compost bin and cycle a lot. As a younger man I felt like I was destined to disappoint. It wasn't rational, it was in my skin, planted there unintentionally by my mum's struggle.

'Always remember you're special. You shouldn't be here, but you are.' How can you be special if you don't do special things?

I remember getting cross with her once when I had failed some school exam, and not cared but felt guilty for letting her down, and she had said it didn't matter, that fate had something more important planned for me. And I thought, 'I don't even know who fate is,' and I said, quietly, unkindly: 'You know, Mum, I feel as though I am at Wembley Stadium, watching the World Cup Final. It's gone to penalties and it's 45-all, so they randomly select two people from the crowd to take a penalty to decide who will win. And I get chosen – I am special, I am lucky, I am the one. And I am walking up to take my penalty, everyone is watching, you're there with your faith and your pride, and it suddenly occurs to me I am going to miss. Now what I should do is say I don't want to take it, tell them to ask someone else, but in the back of my head, Mum, is your voice, telling me I am special, that this is my chance. And that, Mum, costs us the World Cup.'

On the other hand, if fairy stories are written into your life from the very beginning, then whimsy is always available to you or, if not whimsy, then certainly a tolerance for the unlikely. A faith, perhaps, or a willingness to look beyond the obvious, and maybe in the right circumstances that alone might count for something.

My wife is called Melanie. We have twins, Ira and Faye. I'm probably closest to Faye. It's not that I love her more – I love them both with every fibre of my being – but Faye and I get on brilliantly. We laugh a lot together and while I think Mel and I have been pretty interchangeable in our roles as parents since they were born, it has sort of evolved that Ira tends to gravitate toward his mum and Faye tends to drift toward me. Ira is probably more classically mannish than me. He bumps into the world and expects it to fall over. I get my tendency to negotiate with the world from my own mum, Ira gets his clarity of purpose from Mel. Mel is a solicitor. I am a writer who teaches English part-time because I don't make enough money from writing. I wonder sometimes if there is a part of Ira that is disappointed in me, a part of him that thinks of me as fey or compromised. I have no evidence for that, but I ponder it nonetheless.

Anyway, maybe our family is a cliché. Son drifts toward his mum, daughter drifts toward her dad. Not unheard of is it? Here is the thing. Faye – gorgeous, clever, hungry-for-the-world Faye – announced she was pregnant four weeks before she was due to go to university. It was me she told first. I think it's probably important to notice the first feeling you have when your eighteen-year-old daughter tearfully tells you she is pregnant and has no partner. For me, quite bizarrely, it was, 'I suppose that means she isn't moving a hundred miles away to university yet then.' My first feeling, if I had to give it a name, might be called shock, but there was a lacing of something very like relief running through it.

After that I moved on to the 'who, why and what' stuff; questions that must have seemed to be riddled with discomfort, something that looked like disappointment no matter how much it wasn't meant to be, and a significant distaste for the boy who fathered my surprise impending grandchild.

Faye cried a lot, which really wasn't like her. She was never a very demonstrative child. She hadn't cried much past the age of four and I don't think she ever showed rage. She could show anxiety clearly enough; always licking her dry lips, – pale, holding her thumbs inside the palms of her hand and squeezing until the knuckles went white, but she wasn't much of a crier. When we asked her who the father was she kept saying, 'There isn't one,' which everyone thought was a statement of intent rather than a reporting of the facts. Eventually she told Mel, who told me, that there had been no sex. She said she was willing to take a test. 'A hymen test?' said her mother, surprised to find herself in 1925.

'A lie detector,' said Faye.

She said she had barely kissed a boy and of course the word everyone heard was 'barely'.

'Who was the boy you barely kissed?' asked Mel.

'You're missing the point,' said Faye.

I turned my attention elsewhere. I like to think we have established that I am nothing special, but nor am I a cliché. I did not comb the streets looking for a culprit, nor did I demand a list of all the boys she had ever spoken to. I believed her (by belief I mean I chose to trust her rather than test it against reason) when she said she had not had sex. It was, after all, a story I had heard before, and as belief can warp even the clearest of minds this led me – fathers are always two short steps from being ridiculous – to the internet, where I sought out evidence of pregnancy by alternate means, or by shared gym equipment, or towels. There was none. Well, there were one or two wild claims from the state of Kentucky, but nothing I felt I could align with.

The searching I did was at two or three in the morning. I wasn't looking for anything real; I don't think I was even looking for something that would prove her honest and true to a judging world. I didn't care what the world thought, I cared how she felt, and, if nothing else, I wanted her to feel trusted. I thought about all the things that she needed and I decided the thing she needed most was faith. So I was looking for the sake of looking, because it showed her – albeit vaguely, awkwardly, in a dad-dancing sort of way – that I was on her side.

After a little while I turned my quiet attention to drugs. Reason demanded it, I'm afraid. How long does Rohypnol stay in the system? It was too late to test her blood, but it made a kind of sense, of the situation if not of the world. It made the world seem without sense, beyond ridiculous, and darker than I wanted to believe it to be. I instinctively looked to mimic good sense, so I said to Mel that Sherlock Holmes thing about 'when all the impossible things are eliminated the possibility remaining, no matter how unlikely, is the truth'. A smug truism, really, but I said it because it meant Faye wasn't a liar, and also that we didn't have to report her pregnancy to the Vatican.

So the fact that she had been drugged became the story. The police were told. Mel insisted. She said we had a responsibility, or at least it was our story. Faye was immune to it. She didn't need a story. The police were non-committal but agreed that bad men did bad things with bad drugs far more than ordinary people realised. There was little they could do, of course, without Faye remembering anything or being able to suggest where the drugging may have taken place. But they would issue warnings, be drug-vigilant, talk to young people, look at young men even more suspiciously, stop and search. And go home and tell their daughters to be careful.

Anyway, we got through it. Frankly, if an unexpected grandchild is your biggest problem life is treating you okay. And my worry, that there would be a sense that we were colluding with a deceit, letting her lie when she didn't need to, and making the house a dishonest one; well, that didn't happen. We found our way. Ira went to university two hundred miles away, but whenever he came back he was a very good young uncle, and Mel was in her element. As she liked to say, it took her mind right off the menopause.

Six years later and Faye is in the final year of her English degree. She started late, when her little boy, Samuel, was two. She has a boyfriend who is a bit older than her and who dotes on Samuel. His name is John and I know that he and Faye talk a lot about what Samuel should call him. She has friends, plans; she wants to get into book-editing. She knows it won't make her rich, but she has always been good at correcting stories, or the way stories are told. When she was a kid and I would make up rambling tales of a heroine called Faye, she was quick to correct me if I took a wrong turn or used a word that made her ears itch.

She went to a local university so she could live at home, and Mel and I could help with childcare. She has the same best friend she always had. His name is Luke; a pretty, gay, coffee-shop barista who loves to dance and whom Faye has known since infant school. I like Luke. Indeed, if I am honest, I like him more than John whom I find a bit self-consciously quiet and conservative. Luke tells me about new bands he thinks I might like and often I do. I tell him about long-forgotten indie bands he might be interested in and invariably he is. He wants to be a writer and he has shown me some of his stories because people round here still call me a writer, even though I feel like a former writer who reads a lot. He writes nicely enough, compact and direct. He often writes about the space between things and people rather than writing about things and people. I like that. Mind you, I haven't published any fiction in years and if the novel I am working on went any slower I would start moving backwards in time, so frankly, who cares what I think? Still, Luke listens to me, which feeds the illusion that I have to say something as we chat and play with Samuel.

He showed me the beginning of a story he was playing with. Something about a successful gay dancer who, following what he described as 'a thing' with a married man, decides to become a monk. 'I haven't decided if he hurts his ankle and can't dance or if he has an existential crisis about the place of dance in a world where people don't actually give a toss about dancing unless some third-rate celebrity is doing it badly on the BBC...' He blushed. I did say I liked him.

'So, what sort of story is it?' I asked. 'Is our dancer removing himself from the physical world as a retreat into his inner self or is it a bit more Whoopi Goldberg? Will he get the other monks dancing?' I smiled. 'Because there is a film right there, although he probably won't stay a monk at the end. Or if you want a cinema release, still be gay.'

Luke smiled. 'It's a mood piece, which is my way of saying I wrote it quickly after a particularly embarrassing crush fizzled out a couple of months ago.'

'And you toyed with the monastery?'

'Metaphorically.' There was a silence; comfortable, friendly. I knew we were both thinking about Faye because we were both looking at Samuel. I said, 'She's doing okay, I think?'

It was a generous question for a father to ask his daughter's best friend to reassure him. I asked because I wanted to flatter him. To his eternal credit he gave me a gift of sorts in return.

'Can I tell you something? Something ridiculous and lovely about your daughter. Please?'

I nodded. I think I muttered, 'Of course.' I thought she might have helped a limping puppy or joined a choir. But he told me instead about a trip that he and Faye had taken to the seaside.

'We went to Brighton a few years ago, Faye and me. I always believe that to love someone properly you have to be drawn to their smell. She smelt like a girl and that wasn't for me but I would have told her anything and she was the same with me. That's proper love, I think. But it's never been romantic. I think that's why we trust each other so much. There is nothing to distract us from liking each other.

'Brighton was meant to be my kind of place – the gay capital of the UK and everything. The lazy assumption is that as soon as a gay man gets off the train Divine comes on the loudspeaker and the Village People start a parade. I'm not the sort of boy to draw much attention and I didn't feel as though I'd arrived at the Mothership or anything like that. I'd just come to the beach with my friend to eat crepes and go on the water flume before she went to uni. Anyway, at some point that day I said something silly about her forgetting me when she went away, because when people become full of new things old stuff gets squeezed out, you know? I called it the logistics of managing full skin. She laughed and said that was ridiculous and that she was prepared to put on weight, just for me. Anyway, we hugged and then we ate a load more crepes.

'Later we went to see the palm reader on the Palace Pier. But Faye said she didn't really want to know her future. She said that was the point of futures, that you try to negotiate them, not have them presented to you. So I offered my hand and said something like, "Can you offer me any tall dark strangers please?"

And the palm reader said: "They will come whether I see them or not," and smiled.

'She was good. If you go into one of these booths laughing at yourself for being there but having paid nonetheless you are relying on the person in there to turn it into an event. The best way they can do that, I think, is to engage you with a surprise. She was talking to me, but she kept looking at Faye, like she was really curious. She said something generic to her, about how her grandmother loved her or something, and Faye was like, "Well yeah, it's what grandmothers do". She looked me up and down and said: "Please stop fidgeting, you're not in a dance studio now." I confess I lapped that up. I may have said: "How could you know?", all the time believing it obvious. Imagining I was wearing a studio T shirt or pumps. I remember she smiled. Because finally her eyes rested on Faye, even though it was me sitting in front of her with my palm in her hands. She stopped smiling.

'But she kept staring at her, and said, "I see a baby." Then she looked at me and added, "Who'd have thought?"'

He sounded apologetic. Embarrassed that he was telling me about his weekend away; his story, my daughter's life. He looked away and sighed. Samuel was at the other end of the room, completely engrossed in a complicated game involving fifteen matchbox cars and a cave made from cushions.

'Anyway, Faye had had enough at that point, and she left. "A baby what?" I said, but the look on her face made me a bit uncomfortable and it made Faye turn and leave.

'I caught up with her and she looked all teary, she was standing at the end of the pier, looking out to sea like Meryl bloody Streep in that film about the French Lieutenant. I asked her what was up. She was a bit teary. "I'd love a baby," she said. Which shocked me. She'd never said that before. And she wiped her eyes and said: "I know, bloody ridiculous, isn't it?"

'Later on, she said she had a tummy ache, like really bad cramps or something. She blamed the crepes. So we went back to our Bed and Breakfast and she was sick, then we laid on the bed and held hands, and she talked about always secretly wanting to have a baby but not really being the sort of girl who did that. "Have sex?" I asked. "No," she said really seriously. "My cliche is the hard-working girl getting into Cambridge from an average comprehensive school. Not the middle-class girl falling pregnant at eighteen one. Girls can only be one thing at a time, Luke. It's like the law."

'And that,' he said, staring at me as impassively as he could, 'is a true story.'

Samuel was crashing cars into cushions and the sound effects were getting louder. Luke got down on the floor and crawled over to him saying, 'That's no way to treat a scatter cushion, Sammy boy.'

I watched and smiled. Samuel doesn't want for attention, I thought. And Faye doesn't want for love.

I didn't think about the mechanics of what Luke had said. Not the way one might imagine, anyway. I wasn't forensically unpacking the story for a clue to what happened when the lights went out. I just found myself feeling a little bit tearful and a little bit sick. And I was thinking about my mum.

Samuel had reorganised his game and his cars and his cushions. Luke stood up and came back to the sofa opposite where I was sitting.

'Do you think Faye was drugged?' I asked

He smiled. 'No.'

'Why not?'

'Because I was at the things she was at. Our world was never like that. But I know that's what you think.'

I noticed the feeling before the thought, just like when she had told me she was pregnant. It told me I didn't think that at all. That was just a story; somewhere to rest our surprise and our trust and our love and our forgiveness and our acceptance. And I didn't think it was gypsies or God or Luke either.

'I'll think whatever my daughter needs me to think,' I said.

Unconditional love makes you generous doesn't it? Or at least it should, otherwise you don't really do it justice. I suspect I thought of my mother's need to share her inner world as a burden I had to somehow take responsibility for, or at the very least that I needed to hold as lightly and as stoically as I could. Or, more simply, something I needed to look after for her, something that she needed to put into the world that made her unique. Unsilenced her. So later that evening I did that very thing. I sat down with Faye and I told her about her Nan and her immaculate conception. 'Did you believe her?' she asked.

I was probably a bit too arrogant to notice that my responsibility to be special was no more pressing than anyone else's. Perhaps my uniqueness came more passively than I ever imagined. Maybe I am just the man who joins up the generations; a connector between mother and daughter. I realise now that that means I never had to actually do anything more than be a son and later a father, preferably a decent one.

If my mother or my daughter had shouted too loudly about miracles they would be considered mad. They would be drugged or mocked or both. And so if there is madness here I'll own it. Name me deluded, or naive or foolish. I'll be the person saying ridiculous things, not them.

For the record, the reason I am writing this down is because I probably won't live to see if Samuel grows up to have a daughter. But if he does and he finds himself surprised by an immaculate conception I want to be able to tell him not to be afraid. Try to be nice, love well, and be assured that that sort of thing runs in the family.

Cats and Consequences or, if you prefer, Revenge of the Cats

I LIKED HER. I didn't love her. Might I have loved her in time? It is possible, but you know that skip in the heart you get when you are in the space between standing and falling? I didn't get that. I felt curious, even intrigued, but I also had a sense of her as brittle and that makes you wary, doesn't it? I instinctively felt I should be careful. I was right, wasn't I?

She told me that sex with me was her first time. She was twenty-nine. That felt like a hell of a big thing. I don't have a sense of myself as being someone that somebody like her would be saving themselves for. I barely feel like 'the one' in my own life, let alone in anyone else's. And twenty-nine? Had she been in a coma? Part of some weird sect? 'Was it a religious thing?' I asked. She laughed. 'Good lord, no,' she blushed.

I looked at her. I was waiting for more, and that embarrassed her further, I think.

Finally, she laughed and said, 'Can we put it down to having been busy and not make a big deal about it?'

She was twenty-nine, pretty, clever, probably not a psychopath, so how could she not have had a few relationships, or at least one relationship, or the odd, you know, encounter?

When she put her arms around me she held me like someone who didn't know how to be with someone else's skin, which made sense but it wasn't endearing. If I was falling in love it would have been, wouldn't it? She was self-conscious too, guessing how to be, enacting things she had seen or imagined but was not actually connected to. I was very careful, as if she were delicate, which of course she was. Later, it was more spontaneous. Sex is better when the people involved aren't thinking, isn't it? I think I said that afterwards. She thanked me for the insight. I almost expected her to jot it down in a notebook.

For our second date I went to her house and she did this thing – this weird, ridiculous thing that involved a load of cats. She said she could speak to them and that they spoke back. She asked me to say a number and the damn cats – yes, I know this is absurd – they spelled it out in her back garden. I mean they actually formed the number I said (sixty-two), and sat there looking up at us as we stared out of the window of her back bedroom. A bedroom that was jam-packed with cat ornaments, by the way. They sat there in formation, looking sinister. Like cats. Only clever. At first I thought it was a magic trick, like David Blane or someone, but no matter how clever those people are they don't tend to collaborate with animals, do they? Well, there was that bloke with the tiger, wasn't there? And that didn't end well.

Anyway, it was a date. Why would she do a magic trick on a date? What was it? Show and tell? Later I thought she must have drugged me, which forced me to reconsider the psychopath thing. Ridiculous really, but if I was capable of thinking that she could drug me I already didn't trust her, did I? And all those cat ornaments? I felt dangerously close to being in *The Wicker Man*. Only with cats.

That night ended badly. We slept together but it felt clumsy and artificial. I left early the next day and when I saw her at work she was someone else; cool, distant, uninvolved. Very professional. And she didn't talk to me, which made talking to her difficult. She behaved as if nothing had happened and I thought well, you are the doctor, I suppose if it got around that you slept with one of the staff nurses that might make you feel uncomfortable or exposed. So, what is the best thing to do? Say nothing. Be discreet. Pretend nothing happened. I followed her lead and if I am honest the problem was not one of unresolved emotion or on-going desire. It was about social skills. Or at least it was at the beginning.

I left that job about six months later. She didn't come to my leaving do. I would have been surprised if she had. It was a nice, typically hedonistic departure. I slept with a staff nurse called Juliet. We had been flirting for about four months in an almost pantomime sort of way; self-mocking, exaggerated, distracting. You do that sort of thing in that type of environment sometimes. The idea always seemed to be to try to make each other laugh rather than to try to go to bed. Still, it was happy hour and we were both single, so go to bed we did. And that was when it started.

We went back to her place. She had a cat. I didn't think too much about it but if I were a different sort of man, let's face it, I had a bloody good cat story to share. Of course I didn't, it would have been disrespectful and I'm not. Anyway, we didn't need stories or anything. We just went to bed. When we woke up the next morning her cat was sitting on the end of the bed staring at me. He looked cross. I don't think I knew that cats could look cross.

She said his name was Oliver. She said that he was never indoors in the morning. She got out of bed, picked him up and carried him to her living room and all the time he was looking at me. She came back, closed the bedroom door and as we wrapped ourselves around each other I could hear him scratching to get back in. That evening, at home, I was making something to eat. It was a Sunday. I was just relaxing, watching some TV, thinking of an early night with a book, when I heard this howling. I looked out of the window and it was a cat, just sitting in the middle of the courtyard outside my fourth-floor flat. It sounded as though it was in pain, or pregnant. Turned out it was calling other cats. As I watched, and bear in mind I live in a block of flats on a small estate and I was not the only person peering out of the window, a gang of other cats sauntered up. They sat down near the first. They didn't howl, they just sat. And they were all looking up at my flat. There were nine cats staring up at my flat while one of them howled like a drunken fox on a karaoke machine.

It was very hard getting to sleep that night. The cats seemed to take it in turns. The first person threw something out of their window at them at around quarter past one. It was a shoe. I saw it the next morning on the way to work, by which time the cats had gone. It was one of several shoes. There were two books as well. Someone threw water, that stopped them for about ten minutes. I didn't throw anything. I didn't want to draw any more attention to myself.

The next night they were back. Same thing. Shrill, high-pitched, much louder than one would imagine animals that size could be. I think they were working as a team. By the end of the week people in my block had called a tenants' meeting to discuss the cat issue. I didn't go. I had got it into my head that the other people would blame me, know that the cats were here because of me and Nina, which was ridiculous. And yet the idea was in my head, planted like a seed, from the first time Oliver stared at me. It was in my head that this recurrent howling was the revenge of the cats. Which was not fair. I hadn't done anything to them.

A few days later I was out running along the river, which leads in toward the edge of a hill. Sometimes I run up the hill and pretend I am Sylvester Stallone in *Rocky*. The river is narrow there. Shortly afterwards it becomes little more than a trench and there is a footbridge. I sometimes use it as a marker for where I turn back. I look at the hill, tap the railings on the side of the bridge, turn around and head home. Today I jogged half-heartedly a little way up the hill and then turned. I wasn't feeling very dynamic. I ran back along the path with trees on my left and the water on my right. It was sunny, there was little breeze, and it was quiet. I noticed some movement in front of me and thought it was a bird. I was surprised to see, as I drew nearer, that it was a cat. Actually, it was several cats. Solitary creatures, my arse. There were eight of them, spread out trying to look nonchalant and menacing at the same time. Like it was *West Side Story*. With cats.

My first instinct was to slow down but I thought, they are cats, what are they going to do? How can I be intimidated by cats? And more importantly, because obviously a lot of what was happening here was in my head, why would I choose to collude with the probably absurd belief that the cats of Sussex were systematically ganging up on me? And so I carried on running. Well, jogging. I tried to jog nonchalantly, as if they weren't there, but as I got nearer they seemed to move closer together. Not really close, as if they were forming some sort of wall; I could have managed that, I would have jumped the cats. Rather, they moved almost randomly, in such a way as to make it impossible to get past without risking treading on one of them. Or falling in the river. Actually, and I had not noticed this before, cats can be quite scary. I remember seeing something on the internet once where a woman in a bad mood had been kicking snow at a cat. The cat seemed to try to ignore her at first, but you got the sense it was getting annoyed. And then suddenly it jumped up and attacked her face, or at least her head. Cats aren't stupid, this one went for the eyes. I counted the cats as I drew near: there were ten cats. They could, I decided, have me if they wanted to.

So I slowed and stopped. I walked for a few paces and decided – or my body decided and I made up some reasoning for it afterwards – to run back to the hill, cross over the river on the small bridge, and run back along the other side. As I ran back I worried in case they could find a way across the river. What if they had a boat? And, of course, I also realised that the cats had won, and that they would always win.

Over the next few weeks I began noticing two things. First, there are more cats in the city than you think, and a lot of them look at you. Secondly, I had begun wondering about leaving Sussex, moving somewhere else, up north maybe. Of course there would still be cats but even if Nina could speak to cats and had told them to harass me, and even if the cats had spread the word to other cats, it is not as if they have phones or write letters, is it? I mean, could the cats in the south tell the cats in the north? Would the cats in the north do what they were asked by the southern cats? Maybe they were a different tribe? Maybe the north-south divide applied to cats?

One night I was coming home from a late shift, walking the relatively short distance from the train station to my flat, when I got it into my head that I was being followed. I turned around and there was a ginger cat, quite big, quite bold, quite fluffy, walking along behind me. When I stopped, it stopped. When I carried on walking, so did the big fluffy cat. Of course I was nervous, but I didn't run, and I tried to keep the same pace. Apart from anything else I didn't think I could outrun a cat. And if anyone saw me being chased by a cat it would look stupid.

I stopped turning around – I didn't want Ginger Cat to think I was anxious – but I did get out my phone and text Juliet. Since my leaving do we had seen each other a few times, nothing serious but fun nonetheless, and we were both prone to a little spontaneity. I asked if she was doing anything. She replied straight away and said no and that she had a day off tomorrow, which I thought was encouraging. I said, 'Want to come over?'

She replied, 'On my way.'

In some ways I think that text exchange saved my life, or at least my sanity. Juliet arrived at my flat five minutes after me. She lived close, she drove, and she found me standing outside the ground-floor entrance to my block of flats, afraid to move and staring at about twenty-three cats who gathered around the communal entrance. Most of them were sitting and staring, but some of them were prowling.

'Cats hate me,' I said to Juliet when she arrived.

'Cats are weird, aren't they?' she said. 'Well, some cats, not Oliver obviously.' She took me by the hand and we walked toward the door. We picked our way through the herd. Yes, herd. They didn't hiss, they didn't fuss, none of them jumped on my face. They were gone in the morning and were quiet throughout the night.

Later I told Juliet I was toying with the idea of moving. 'Why?' she asked.

'Too many cats,' I said, trying to make it sound like a joke.

She snuggled into my chest and laughed. 'Well,' she said, 'if you do, we'll visit if you want.'

'Who's we?'

'Me and Oliver, of course. I think he quite likes you even if the other cats don't.'

I liked Juliet, particularly when she was close to naked. And even when she wasn't, she made me smile, and I felt nice when we were together. I imagined that if I did move to the north it would be nice if she visited, and I would miss her if she didn't. Yet all the time I was noticing this, as I was inhaling the smell of her, and lightly stroking her straight blonde hair, I realised that another thought was tumbling in like a clumsy burglar. If I moved north and I wanted to stay in touch with Juliet, and it felt as if I did, then I would have to tell her that Oliver couldn't visit. Not that I thought she was serious about bringing him with her. I mean, who brings their cat on romantic weekends? In fact, who takes their cat anywhere other than the vet's once a year? And then I noticed that this other thought kept coming, rolling toward the front of my head like a migraine or boulder. I physically turned away from it but it edged further in anyway. What, I found myself thinking, if Juliet is somehow in on it?

Healing Hands, Burning Bridges

I AM PART of a community of charlatans. We live in a large, old farmhouse in Wales. There is a dip in the kitchen floor and a hole in the living-room wall that we have stuffed with newspaper and an old sheet. It could probably benefit from a coat of paint, but it is home to nearly two dozen of us, if you include the caravans outside.

There are people here who claim to have magic hands, and others who believe they can cure pretty much any illness by offering advice on the wearing of what they describe as 'your spirit colours', in the right combination, of course. They ask you a lot of questions about yourself to discover your spirit colours and they often have to touch you when you are nearly naked as well. It is a serious business. They are not, after all, simple fashion advisors. This place is full of hippies, dreamers, misfits, and maybe even the odd con artist. We have Chakra hunters, needle wielders, herb-gathering psychotics, crystal-waving new-agers and drummers. We have two sodding drummers!

And then there is me. I am real, totally demonstrably and unsettlingly real. This is as good a place to hide that fact as any.

My name is Susan. I am sixty-four and, as the beautiful robot in that dark, rainy film said, 'I have seen things you people would not believe.'

I know exactly where my powers came from. I inherited them from my mother. She told me when I was seven, and I was cross with her for a week. I remember that she told me I was special. I sort of knew that the way I like to think most seven-year-olds know it. I think if you feel loved as a child – and of course being loved is about being seen in soft focus every day, isn't it – then you feel special. Beyond that, special meant different, and I am not sure I ever wanted that. I know lots of children do. I don't think I ever did.

I healed my History teacher when I was eleven. I did it in front of people. I had to. He was a good man and he had risked his life to save me and my friend Nancy from a terrible fire, and my mother told me I could. I held his charcoaled, ruined flesh until it regrew, and then I went home and had ice cream and tinned peaches as if it was my birthday.

The strange thing about that public healing was that afterwards nobody spoke about it. Not directly. Nobody shouted 'witch' or 'angel'. Nobody asked me later to heal their aching feet or rub their eyes so they wouldn't need glasses anymore. Nobody cried 'miracle'. Even Mr Styles never said anything explicit, although he did say 'thank you' when he gave me back my homework a year later, and I wanted to say, 'It's only homework, Sir.' Or 'Was it that good?' And try to get a laugh from the class, but after he released my book he turned his hand over to show it had no scars, no burns, and I thought he might cry so I held his gaze for as long as I could and said very quietly, 'No, Sir, thank you.' And neither of us ever said another word about it.

But of course, things did change for me after that. I was treated a little differently, a bit like a princess from another country. There was something vaguely respectful in the space people offered me when they were near, but it was wrapped in caution. Nobody had shouted 'witch', but the possibility that I was one had entered into the collective consciousness of the school. Surprisingly nobody mocked me. Perhaps they thought I would turn them into a frog.

Or perhaps they sensed something that was truly important, perhaps even sacred.

I think it was expected that I would go on and do well, whatever that means. I was a good student, everybody said so. Medicine at one of the good universities beckoned. But I left school at fifteen and got a job in a shop. I didn't want to be a doctor. The very idea annoyed me. I had an unfair advantage. My talent belittled learning and paradoxically it felt as though it limited the things available to me. It may have been teenage hormones, of course, but I felt that my power offered me less of the world than was available to other people. And I learnt quite early that I couldn't mend myself.

Of course working in the shop didn't last. These hands could not just hand over fudge and tobacco for long.

I started going to night school. I studied Philosophy and English, and I carried on studying those subjects at university when I finally went at twenty-one. My mother was very proud, although I think she would have been proud no matter what I did. She treated my gift like a clubfoot; a distinguishing feature rather than a defining quality. All she had to do was look at me and I felt safe, which is perhaps why she is the only person I ever gave myself permission to be angry with.

She got ill while I was away at university and didn't tell me. My father said it was because she felt that it had taken me a while to start living and she didn't want me to stop because of her. I told him that I could have healed her, why didn't she let me do that? He shook his head. 'She couldn't be healed. She knew that.'

I didn't even countenance forgiving my mother for dying, and I suspect I acted that out over the next five or six years. I knew a lot of angry people then. Some of them took drugs, some of them were joylessly promiscuous, some railed against governments or wars. Me? I gorged myself on healing strangers.

It started, as everything did in those days, in the pub. I had a few drinks one night with friends from university, and without thought or plan I told them I had to go and do something quite important. I may have slurred my words. I remember bumping into a table as I left the pub; it left a bruise on my thigh that later turned a deep bluey-yellow colour. I walked through the town centre in the rain. I was soaking when I got down to the hospital, and my then black hair was dripping on the floor. I must have looked homeless or lost. I probably smelt of beer, but I walked into the A&E department and quietly and damply went around the waiting room healing people. I had to do it when the doctors and nurses weren't looking, obviously. I mended a broken ankle, a dislocated shoulder, a chest infection, and made a migraine go away. I told the people I helped not to say anything about me, and they didn't.

I tried to do the same thing a couple of weeks later at a different hospital, but someone told the local paper about this healer who made her husband walk after he'd been hit by a taxi on the high street, and the ambulance people said he may have broken his back. He hadn't, but healing a ruptured disc is pretty significant if it is your disc. Still, the local paper went to town on it and it didn't feel safe to do it again. Anyway, it didn't feel like enough. Mum had told me not to overdo the healing when I was young and had helped my friend Nancy when she had fallen over and grazed her knee. 'Why?' I asked. 'Does it run out? Can I use it all up if I'm not careful?' She shook her head. 'It can take you over,' she said quietly, 'and that can stop you having the life you need, sweetheart.'

This made no sense to me, until healing a casualty department full of sick people felt unsatisfying and I got the idea to maybe go to Vietnam while America was still bombing it.

Of course there were no flights to Vietnam, it being ripped apart by a war and everything, but I quite fancied healing gunshot wounds, drawing bullets from bloody holes, stemming the bleeding from blown-away limbs. I wondered how far I could go. I remember wondering if I could regrow legs the way I knew I could regrow skin, whether I could replace blackened lungs or malfunctioning livers, whether I could make the blind see.

I never made it to Vietnam. If I had I would not be telling you this story from a commune in Wales. I went to Northern Ireland for a month. I didn't heal anybody. I just heard a lot of shouting. It annoyed me in a way it shouldn't have, so I came back again and signed up to do a Masters degree and kept my eye open for a war zone. Or even a small natural disaster.

Instead I met a man who I loved. His name was Steven and I notice that when I look back on him and his impact on my life I think in clichés like 'he took me out of myself' and 'I learnt as much about myself when he held me as I did when he let me down'. I suspect I think those things in order to not think anything else.

In truth he was a give-way sign. He slowed me down and made me look both ways; instead of simply staring at what happened when I did what I did in the world I had to notice what happened when the world did what it did to me. I needed that and perhaps I confused that with thinking that I needed him.

He slept with a friend of mine at university and that hurt me so very much. We had been a small band of

131

mature students who imagined we had more refined rules of engagement because we were between 23 and 30, Steven being the oldest. We didn't. He married her in the end, which should have made me feel better, that it wasn't just a fling, but it didn't.

I moved on anyway, and I did find my Vietnam, my disaster, although it wasn't exactly natural. I was at a country fair with a man I was seeing. It wasn't serious, but it is nice to have someone to be with outside in the summer. He had floppy brown hair and wore baggy cream-coloured trousers. He was called Andrew. If it weren't for the balloon story I would probably have forgotten him by now.

It was one of those quietly idiosyncratic English events we had before they invented Health and Safety. A large field, home-made cakes. The nearest city was Canterbury, which wasn't really a proper city, more a town with a big church. Local people sold pies. Other local people sold dope. We drove down from London because Andrew lived in Herne Bay and knew about this quaint fair which had a tombola and large steam-rollers you could sit in, and a hot-air balloon that would take you for a ride for less than £1.

Andrew and I were sitting on the grass sharing a piece of cake. He was talking about work. He did something to do with money or insurance or banks. I never really understood, or cared. I was trying to decide whether I slept with him because I liked him or whether I liked him only because I enjoyed sleeping with him. I remember I was thinking about it in the way you think about crossword puzzles before you decide if you are going to get your pen out.

He had asked me if I wanted to go on the balloon but I said no. It didn't look safe and I didn't like heights. But we sat and watched it come and go a couple of times. It is a funny thing, watching a hot air balloon take off. It seems so uncertain. The basket that people stand in – I still don't know what that is called – it looks surprised when it lifts off the ground. And it creaks, like it is being woken up when it doesn't want to be.

Anyway, we saw a family queuing to get in; three kids and their parents. This was clearly what they had come for and the middle child, the only boy, was so excited I thought he needed sedation. He was probably seven or eight, and as they waited to get in he couldn't keep any of his limbs still. He was hopping from foot to foot and throwing his arms about like a drummer or a bad fighter. The oldest daughter was trying to be mature, but she looked excited too. The youngest girl looked nervous, scared even. She clung to her father's hand and he looked as though whatever she felt was contagious. He may have wondered what he was doing, taking his family up into the sky in a balloon from a field in Kent, although I probably only imagine that in retrospect. He was a well-dressed man with a boxy jacket and loose-fitting trousers. He had very neat black hair. He looked debonair, which made me assume the mother did most of the work. The children's mother looked happy to have a few minutes to herself. I remember that, before the basket left the ground, she was waving and smiling, pausing only to take a cigarette from her handbag and light it with a long exhalation of relief.

Of course, we didn't know what a safe balloon flight looked like, not really. It left the ground slowly and the children squealed with something like delight, although I remember thinking that it must be a unique feeling for a child, being elevated slowly beyond your own height, and then the height of your parents, your house, your expectation. I think I heard the basket creak as it lifted off the ground. I imagined that taking off would be the challenge, and my interest reduced as the balloon went higher. But I still noticed a listing when it got to maybe fifty or sixty feet up, and I noticed the balloon didn't look like it did in the pictures. It was not symmetrical. It looked to be straining.

Two of the ties that bound the balloon to the basket had frayed and the basket on one side began to dip. The movement alarmed the children and they dipped with the basket. Their father moved to them and suddenly all of the weight was at the weakest part of the connection between balloon and people and that accentuated the tilt. The older girl, disadvantaged by her height which made the edge of the basket a hurdle rather than a barrier, was the first to fall. Arguably she was lucky as she fell from only seventy or eighty feet up, but she didn't fall well. Leading with her head, she turned over and landed nearly on her back. Her mother threw her cigarette down and screamed. The girl's body made an awful thumping noise as it hit the grass below. Some people ran toward her but most looked upward, looking for something that explained away what had just happened, or threatened worse to come.

My first thought was that I could help the girl if I could get to her before too many other people. I stood up, started walking quickly toward her and said, 'I can help.' Andrew may have asked, 'How?' but I was halfway toward her. By the time I arrived, at least half a dozen people had gathered and plenty more were coming. I didn't have the sense that they were doctors – they looked confused and worried rather than concentrated and working – so I said, 'I'm a doctor, let me help please.'

Now I don't imagine for a moment that they thought I was a doctor, but nobody was going to say, 'Are you? You look very young to be a doctor.' Or, 'Show us some credentials,' unless they were a doctor. Someone said, 'I'll get some hot water,' but that translates as 'I don't know what to do and I don't want to be near this so will go and get some random things on the off-chance someone is going to have a baby or need a cup of tea'.

The girl was unconscious. Her back had snapped, her arm was broken, her hip and pelvis fractured. She had a brain injury from landing on her skull and she had blood leaking from her spleen. I put one hand on her head and one on her back, and her mother arrived as I did so. I glanced up at her and I thought for a moment she was going to scream at me to let go, to step back to let her hold her child, but she saw something in my eyes, a certainty perhaps that helped her hold herself. Someone said, 'She's a doctor,' but the mother didn't listen. She just looked at me, perhaps because she could not look at her daughter.

I felt the bone repair, like the shadow of a snake under skin. I felt the body move back toward itself and I saw the child's arm move in acceptance.

I exhaled like I was blowing away the wreckage and I lent across her and placed both hands on her head. I held her with my thumbs just under her eyes and I felt her heal in my fingers. I held her still and I paused to hear her breathe. She coughed, opened her eyes, rolled over, and was sick on the grass.

Her mother looked at me like I was an angel or a witch. She was feeling too much for me to be able to tell which and those are the words I have come to ascribe to others who I imagine describe me to themselves. Whatever she named me, I know that she would have given her life in gratitude at that moment. I nodded. I wanted to share a moment, I think, as a woman with another woman, over a daughter, but there was another scream and I heard someone say, 'Oh dear God, no.'

The balloon had carried on going up with the balloonist struggling to keep some sort of control. He wanted some elevation and he had got it, to his credit. The balloon was high, too high to see the people in it clearly, although looking up one had the sense of a father holding his two children very tightly and maybe swearing at the man in charge.

But the balloon was struggling to do what it was meant to do. It existed to form an elevator to the clouds and a platform upon which to view the ground. But it was, at heart, an awful lot of fabric with a fire underneath it. It relied on the right connections, and those connections had failed. One half of the balloon looked to be emptying, which was not possible really. The lines had changed the direction of the hot air, causing the balloon to list more and more until it stopped being controlled by the balloonist and instead accelerated in the wind away from the field. People tried to run after it but it was going too fast. Others got in their cars, but it was 1974, not 1924, and fields had fences and dips and trees and balloons, even ones which are out of control, do not have to negotiate such things.

We all saw the balloon dip. I heard someone mutter, 'Jesus Christ' in response to it accelerating toward the ground, giving up on its balloon-ness, handing itself over to gravity. It was just a thing that didn't belong in the sky, falling, with people in it. It was too far away for us to hear if anyone screamed.

People began running toward it before it landed, and we kept running after it was out of sight. It came down in a small group of trees. Arguably the trees broke its fall, although I suppose hitting heavy branches from a great height doesn't function as too much of a cushion. I imagine as the ground drew nearer the children's father, whose name was Frank Wright, must have considered the trees a bigger threat than the ground, because it was clear from his body that he used himself as a shield and held his kids under him. I think he, or the basket at least, must have collided full on with the trunk of the largest tree. I think it killed him instantly. It certainly broke his back in half, and his head was not facing in a direction heads can face in. The impact must have turned the basket, aided no doubt by what was left of the balloon catching on the upper branches and acting as a faulty parachute. This meant that Frank Wright did protect his children to some extent as the basket hit the ground, side on, and kept going. Wright was certainly dead long before the basket stopped moving and his body trapped his daughter in the corner, which saved her, but also squashed her. She had two compact fractures, concussion and, most unpleasantly, her father's hand had caught under her and she had bounced on it so hard and with so much force his thumb had caught between her ribs, stabbing her bluntly and hooking her to his broken body.

The boy had been protected from the first impact by his dad but was thrown clear as the basket turned and bounced a few times before landing on above-ground tree roots and broken branches. He had a smashed eye socket, and at first sight we could not see if he had an eye in it. He also had a punctured lung, a fractured skull, some broken ribs. He should have died too.

His mother got to the wreckage before I did. As I entered the copse, she came for me, her hands taking one of mine. she wanted to speak but couldn't. She led me to the boy. There were others there but she pushed them away and ushered me forward while the other people stood back. Nobody said a word.

I put one hand over his eyes and the other on his ribs. It was his lung I looked to first, but I could feel the swelling on his head reduce and I felt the faintest flicker of eyelashes on my palm. I imagined my right hand hovering over his lung and the lung inflating itself. I imagined the broken bones remembering how they had been when they danced with excitement. I healed him more quickly than I had ever healed anyone. I heard him say, 'Mummy.' I may have felt faint. I may have just been noticing the eyes around me and acknowledging the drama.

'Please. Please,' the mother said. Her name was Fiona. I imagine that I would not have liked her if I had met her in any other circumstances. I think, to my shame, I would have thought her bourgeois. Whatever that means. But I liked her now. I liked her very much. She bent down to her son, she stroked his head, she said, 'I love you, oh I love you.' And she said, 'Now your sister, now your father...' and then looking at me directly she said 'please' again.

I didn't even bend down to touch Frank Wright. I may have sounded cold when I said, 'I'm sorry, there is nothing.' I heard her make a noise like a kitten makes when it wants food, but when I turned my attention to the youngest child she did too.

When I saw the thumb and the hand in the girl's side I hesitated for a moment. There were people there, maybe seven or eight, and more were coming. Again, the mother said, 'Let her help, please let her help,' and again people stepped aside. I sighed. I may have hesitated. I had had too much time to think. I had been too public, there were opinions forming, people watching, I was a long way from the car. I touched the child's head. There was blood on her brain, a fracture to the skull. I stroked her near her eyes and felt the blood drain, the bone knit. I took Frank Wright's hand as gently as I could, and unhooked it from his daughter's rib. It wasn't hard. It was lifeless, although the hole in her side was bloody. I ran my hand to her ribs, to her leg, to her chest, and I felt her bones slowly mend. And then I thought about the hole in her side. It was big and deep and there was a lot of blood. I sighed. I wondered if I could hear an ambulance, but I couldn't. I turned to Fiona Wright and I said, 'You cannot ever tell. Do you understand?' And she nodded without hesitation, so emphatically she would have given me her life.

'Promise,' I said.

She nodded again. 'I promise,' she said. 'I swear.'

I placed my hand over the wound. It tickled, it may have resisted. I fleetingly wondered for the first time if there was a relationship between what I did and what I felt, but the wonder passed and the wound healed. Skin flowed like milk and then like sand and then like flesh, and she healed, and for me the most remarkable thing was that nobody said a word, nobody who watched made a sound. The girl called for her mother. Her brother walked over, staring at me. As I lifted my head, I could see the older girl walking with some grown-ups. They didn't know they had lost their father.

I stepped toward Fiona Wright and I said, 'I'm sorry for your loss.' I nodded toward her husband's body. I may have slightly shrugged, I don't know.

She whispered, 'Thank you, thank you, thank you.'

I saw Andrew standing with some other men. 'I have to go,' I said. Andrew looked the most uncomfortable person there and I realised it was because he was the one who was leaving with me. For everyone else I didn't need to be real.

The balloon crash made the national news. No film, obviously, but there was a grainy black-and-white photograph of the debris. The balloonist died too. His neck broke with the first impact and, as the balloon descended, he became caught in the trees. I did not even see his body;

it was thirty feet high, hanging from a limb, his hands by his side. I was too tired to look for anyone I was not led to, and nobody led me to him.

The papers all reported the accident too. One of them had it on the front page. The children were described as lucky. They had survived through a miracle and the sacrifice of their father. Nobody mentioned me. No healing was revealed. Fiona Wright kept her word, and everyone else had stayed silent. Perhaps she had asked them, perhaps they had just chosen to be kind, but I felt warm, maybe valued. Like I wasn't a witch.

I set myself up as a healer after that. I had my reservations. For one thing, despite my gift I don't have much time for the industry of magic-handed, weak-minded nonsense that gathers in those alternative health shops. Selling bits of dried flowers and calling it an elixir is hokum. As is a lot of the other made-up silliness people gravitate to because they want gentle things to have meaning. I didn't join one of those. I simply placed an advert in the local paper. I advertised myself as 'Practical Healer'. I didn't want anything to allude to gods or faith or anything too ephemeral. I'm not proud to say that I expected people's despair to get me my first few clients and after that word of mouth would do the rest. That was the case. Unfortunately, this was when things got a bit complicated.

The first person who came to see me was an African woman who brought her child. He was a tiny wee thing with scared eyes and skinny legs. He had rickets, in 1976. I cured him quickly and he smiled. It sounds ridiculous now, but until that child had smiled I had not really felt the joy in what I did. It had somehow been an expression of me or my mood rather than an interaction with the world. I must have decided on some level to do something about that when I opened my business, but I hadn't been conscious of it.

What was striking was that most of my patients during that time were black, Irish, or poor. I think these days so-called alternative health centres attract a different group of people – people who assure themselves that they have choices. My patients came to me because they didn't.

Within three months I had a very steady trade. I saw lots of people and I didn't charge much. I didn't need to. Healing them didn't take long or cost anything, and they didn't have much money to give. I met people I liked, I attended to everything I encountered and at the end of each week people who I had helped would bring me food, or wine, or tickets to the cinema, gifts of thanks or acknowledgement. Things that made me feel almost one of them. I counted how many people I saw in the three-and-a-half years I ran that business. It was over 4,200. A third of those were children. I think I could have stayed there. Sometimes I think I would have liked that.

I was living in Hackney, in London. It was 1980 and it suited me perfectly. It was the most accepting place I had ever lived. It was a good place to heal because it was dense and busy, and people didn't pay much attention to difference. But then I got a little bit above myself. I could tell you stories about my life that have happened since 1980, but they would have a different flavour. I would have a different flavour. On reflection perhaps that is why I am telling what I am telling.

Veronica believed in me with a reverence that I found unnerving and flattering at the same time. She had had breast cancer and I healed her. She ran a market stall in Dalston and she also sang in a ska band. She was very beautiful; thin-faced, coffee-coloured skin, with hyper-alert brown eyes. She laughed more than anyone I had ever known, and if you live in yourself as much as me you can be quite seduced by people who laugh a lot.

Every week Veronica would drop a bag of fruit and veg round at my place. I used to say there was no need, but she shrugged and would say either, 'You saved my life,' or, 'I hate waste,' depending on what mood she was in. Sometimes we would chat about what gigs she had coming up, what we thought of local or emerging bands, or occasionally how I was. I found 'How are you?' eternally unsettling. I tended to always mumble, 'Fine,' without thought the way most people do, but I wasn't avoiding telling people how I was so much as skimming over giving myself any thought at all. Veronica tended to see through that. She would gently mock me. 'Anyone laid their healing hands on you lately?' Or once, 'What do you do that makes you happy, sweetie? Apart from making ill people better? What do you do for you?'

I may have said, 'I love reading,' but the truth was I had stopped reading. I had stopped a lot of things. I tried to help people who came to see me, and beyond that I lived small. I don't know why.

Sometimes Veronica would talk about her life. Her occasional lovers, of both sexes, her hopes and her frustrations with her music, and once or twice about her mother who lived in Southampton and was 'getting a bit batty'. I had no reason to believe those two things were related.

One Friday in September I did what felt like a brave thing. She brought round fruit and I asked her if she fancied a walk in the park for coffee. She said yes. It wasn't a date, I didn't think, but it was quite exciting. I had not initiated anything social for a long time. I hadn't quite worked out how to separate out socialising with people and healing them in the same part of town, and I had quite a deeply-rooted sense of myself as being a secret.

We went to Clissold Park and I bought cake. Veronica knew lots of people, but even though they often seemed to want to stop and talk, she said she had no time, she was with me. I'm not saying it was romantic. Apart from anything else I don't think I had the confidence to think romance was available at that point in my life. But it did feel exciting.

I asked her about her mother. She was quite dismissive at first. She said she was forgetful but that she had always been a little bit 'dotty'. I asked her how she meant, and she told a story about her mum putting the turkey in the oven one Christmas and forgetting to turn it on. There was a pause and Veronica said, 'I think she may be beginning to get dementia.' Without thinking, I said, 'I've never tried to do anything with dementia.'

Veronica's mother was called Elizabeth. She was an Irish immigrant on her third husband. Veronica's father, a Jamaican bass player, had never really settled into family life and had gone back to Jamaica where Veronica had visited him. There had been a brief marriage of convenience to a gay Australian chap who wanted to stay in the country longer than his visa allowed and gave Elizabeth £200 to marry him. He decided to go home six months later and had the cheek to ask for some of the money back. Elizabeth gave him £10 and a divorce.

Elizabeth had been married to Tom, the father of her youngest, for fifteen years. They lived in Southampton and I agreed to go visit with Veronica the following weekend.

'She won't let us share a room,' Veronica said. I blushed and muttered, 'Of course not … I never thought…' and then she kissed me, so softly. So I kissed her back.

It turned out I wasn't able to help Elizabeth. Something happened on the way.

We went down on the train. It was slow and dirty but I quite liked it. Veronica brought fruit. I had made flapjacks. When we got to Southampton station Veronica's brother, or half-brother, was waiting. His name was Mikey. He was young, very quiet. His skin and the shape of his face was the same as Veronica's, but his temperament was quite the opposite. His face was masked and still. Not only did he barely speak, and when he did, he didn't move his lips, but he didn't look as though he ever smiled. He was here to give us a lift, Elizabeth had sent him. This was a good sign, said Veronica. 'It means she hasn't forgotten we're coming.' I liked the fact she said 'we'.

Elizabeth lived in a place called Highfield. It wasn't very far away but it seemed hard to get to despite Mikey's willingness to drive as fast as he could between traffic lights that were only fifty yards apart.

'Traffic isn't usually this bad,' he said quietly.

'See, it talks,' said Veronica. He didn't smile.

We had been in the car for maybe twenty minutes when we saw flashing blue lights up ahead. 'There is the hold-up,' Mikey said. 'If it's the police they will stop us no matter what they are doing.'

'Why?' I said naively.

'Black,' said Veronica, and I blushed.

It wasn't the police. It was a fire engine and an ambulance, and they were attending a car accident.

I had never seen a crashed car before. There is something shocking about folded crushed metal. Cars are symmetrical, solid, reassuring bubbles. When you see them from another car as I did then, one wrapped around a lamppost, the other on its side against a wall, you instantly feel more fragile.

We had to stop. There was a policeman in the road with his hand in the air, and we were maybe fifteen or twenty cars back. I looked at Veronica and shrugged. It felt like a duty. She nodded and we both got out of the car.

'Where you going?' said Mikey.

'To help.'

'They don't need your help…'

But we were gone. When we drew near, I said to the policeman that I was a doctor and wondered if I could help. 'Thanks,' he nodded, letting me past. 'But we need to get them out of the car first.'

The ambulance crew were dealing with a man beside the overturned car. His head was moving as he lay on the floor and he let them talk to him, check him, soothe him. I walked toward the car that surrounded the lamppost. It was an old car even then. A Hillman Imp, red with a black roof. The windscreen was smashed, the post had cut through the engine, and the chassis of the car had been so bent the doors would not open. There were firemen, five of them, with cutting equipment, and there was crying from a child.

'I'm a doctor,' I lied again. 'Can I help?'

One of the firemen, a man of about my age, with hands that looked as if they had an extra coating of skin, glanced up. 'Hello Doc, maybe when we get them out. We nearly have the kid. Little girl.' As he spoke his colleagues were using a metal brace and what looked like the sort of jack you would use to change a tyre to force a gap between the top and bottom of the small broken car. 'Need to cut off her seat belt,' one of them said. You could feel the relief that she had worn one.

They passed her out along a line and one of them called to the ambulance crew, 'Got one for you.'

'She can help,' said Veronica, as the ambulance man came close.

'You a doctor?' he said tonelessly.

'Yeah.'

'Whereabouts?'

'London.'

'UCH?'

'Royal Free.'

'What do you do?'

'Trauma.'

I didn't look at him once as I spoke. All the time I looked at the girl. She was maybe six years old, and crying, which seemed like a good sign. Her right arm was limp, her left leg looked broken. 'Lay her down,' I said. And they did.

She was lucky. She had a dislocated shoulder, a broken leg, badly bruised ribs, and whiplash but it could have been worse. I looked into her eyes and held her head and arm. As the pain left her I saw something, or rather failed to see something, that unnerved me. I expected relief – I always see that. As they are released from whatever pain they are in I see them breathe again. But I didn't see it in her. I said, as quietly as I could, 'Has the pain gone?'

She nodded. I said, 'So why don't you look relieved?'

'Because he'll do it again,' she whispered.

The ambulance man clearly hadn't heard this, as he said, 'Good work, Doc. Not sure what you did, but she's okay.'

There was shouting from near the car. All of the firemen were moving. One of them was inside the car, cutting away at something with a saw. I heard one on the outside say, 'She's a mess, the driver got off better than she did.'

The little girl weakly said, 'Mummy?'

I whispered, 'It's okay, I'll help her. It will be okay.'

'Blimey,' said the ambulance man. 'Not sure what you did, but she's okay.'

I nodded, but I was already looking at the woman. The woman really was a mess. Blood covered half of her face and her black hair was matted to the side of her head. The way the firemen were so tenderly trying to ease her from the car suggested a neck injury. Her body was limp, her eyes closed.

They laid her on a stretcher and one of the ambulance crew began to assess her. He opened her eyes and shone a torch into them, and felt for a pulse in her neck. I moved to the other side of her and I put my hand on her chest. She had been crushed like a concertina, breaking two vertebrae in her neck but not killing her. Her brain was swelling, her liver was bleeding, her pelvis was broken into three pieces. I looked at the ambulance man and said as gently as I could, 'It is good that I am here.' I smiled. He paused long enough for me to put my hands on her head and feel her neck align. The vertebrae touched like reunited lovers and then embraced. I placed the palm of my hand on the front of her head and felt her brain calm. It was like the tide going out on a flat sea. I noticed that she looked a little bit like Veronica – the same colour skin, the same soft hair. I wondered later if that affected me at all. She opened her eyes and exclaimed, 'Amy!'

'She's fine,' I said. 'She is just here, she is fine.'

I placed my hands below her ribs, near her liver, and she inhaled as she healed. As she did so she realised what I was doing, and she raised her hand and held my arm.

'Bobby?'

'They're getting him,' I said. 'He'll be okay.'

She gripped me where she had been holding me. It was instinctive and then it was pleading.

'He did it on purpose. I swear he did. He said if we can't stay together we will go together. He tried to kill us. I swear.' Amy was standing beside me now. Veronica was beside her. The child looked at me, frightened, not relieved.

The ambulance man was staring at me. 'What did you just do?'

'Helped,' said Veronica.

'How?'

I ignored him. I was staring at the woman who was staring back at me. The 'how' didn't feel as though it mattered. For the first time in my life I had become lost in the 'why'.

I heard one of the firemen shout again, 'Here we go, easy, yes.'

I turned to see Bobby being lifted from the car still attached to the seat. He was unconscious, slumped to his right side; a youngish man with short blonde hair and big shoulders.

'She's good!' shouted the ambulance man who had been with me. 'She's very, very good.'

I found myself slowly getting up and moving toward where they set Bobby down, and as they cut away the seat belt I thought, 'What sort of man decides to kill himself and his family in a car crash but puts on a seat belt?' As I drew near to him I could see that he was dazed, conscious, and looking at the woman with something that was not relief or kindness.

'Doc?' said the ambulance man who had followed me over. 'What do you think?'

I bent down and smelt alcohol and cigarettes. I put my hand on his shoulder and he instinctively moved to brush it away.

'She's a doctor,' the ambulance man said, looking at me. I looked back and curled my nose slightly. The ambulance man nodded. He smelt it too. He gave the slightest shrug. He might be arrested later, but first we needed to save him, heal him, restore him. I glanced over my shoulder. I saw the woman and Amy holding each other and I saw Veronica with them. I thought that I wanted to be with them, maybe even be them. I didn't want to be here touching this man. I didn't want this. I put my left hand on his head and my right hand on his sternum. His skull was fractured and his chest battered. He had three, maybe four broken ribs and his lung was punctured. I felt it move to mend under my touch and I pulled my hand away. He winced. He looked at me with dark grey eyes. I had never seen anyone with eyes like that before. I have seen fear and despair in the people I have healed. I have seen suspicion, relief, love and confusion, but not that much rage – so much of it as to transcend his pain.

I touched his head. It was hot and he instinctively pulled away. His brain had collided with his skull. It was bruised and cramped. I could feel it, traumatic brain injury; it would swell, try to burst from its barrel or squash against the sides. It felt to me as if the tissue turned to my touch, like flowers to the rain, waiting to be healed. And as it did so I closed my fingers, I clenched my hand, I drew away.

'Doc?'

I thought of lying. Lying would have worked. I only had to say, 'I think this one is for you,' or, 'I can't feel anything, he needs a scan,' or 'He'll be fine.' Except I couldn't have said the second one. The first was passive, the second would be misdirection, like killing someone. At the time I thought there was a difference, but of course there never was. Not saving someone when you can save them might be different to murder, but only if your heart tells you it is. I didn't speak. I walked away, past the woman and Amy. Veronica followed as I left. It becomes a different type of power when you choose not to use it.

That was over thirty-five years ago. Everything changed then. It is not that I lost my power – it is still with me – but it is not constant. It had been like a beam, but then it became a flickering light. Sometimes it worked, sometimes it didn't. Sometimes it made a fool of me. Veronica said she was proud of me. She said that I chose to be human and my power respected that but didn't want to leave me completely. She said it as she baby-kissed my tummy maybe a year later. She was very patient with me, but I didn't believe I deserved it. In the end I said she didn't have to be grateful for the rest of her life, and I told her to go. She said the best people turn bad things on themselves and stayed.

There was a child who came to my clinic a few years later. He had cancer. Lovely kid, eight years old, big blue eyes, a wise baby face. I tried to help and I couldn't. I wept over that boy as I felt the cells spread across his tiny frame. If I had known what I was losing I would have saved Bobby. Would he have tried again? Would I be responsible for anything that happened to Amy or her mother?

I have other stories. This is the one I choose to tell.

I live in a community of charlatans. I plant vegetables, make cheese. Tell stories to children and occasionally heal people. I like it here. Except for the bloody drummers and the thoughts that come to me in the night.